THE PIECES OF THE PUZZLE

ROBERT STANEK

The Pieces of the Puzzle

Reagent Press LLC

www.**reagentpress**.com

Cover design & illustration by Robert Stanek
ISBN-10: 1-57545-235-9, ISBN-13: 978-1-5754-5235-7

REAGENT PRESS

Also by Robert Stanek

Ruin Mist Chronicles
Keeper Martin's Tale
Kingdom Alliance
Fields of Honor
Mark of the Dragon

Scott Evers Thrillers
The Pieces of the Puzzle
The Cards in the Deck
The Pawns on the Board
The Players in the Game

Absolutes & Other Stories

**Look for spoken-word versions of these
and other Robert Stanek books!**

Chapter 1

Washington, D.C.
Friday, 24 December

Life wasn't a Christmas movie and no one knew that better than Scott Evers as he sat alone on a park bench at 4 a.m. on the morning of Christmas Eve. He held a bottle wrapped in a brown paper bag in his right hand and there was a tiny portable device nearly hidden within his left. A lamppost off to one side of the bench cast his shadow out onto the brown grass of the trash-strewn park. That it hadn't snowed this late in December didn't bother Scott. He thought it was just as well not to have a white Christmas this year.

Two people with strikingly different backgrounds watched him from opposite sides of the square. Neither seemed to know the other was there; rather they simply watched and waited for the moment to make their move.

She was parked in a silver Intrepid. The car, like everything else she possessed, was rented. Tears had washed her mascara halfway down her cheeks, and her hand on the sweated leather of the steering wheel was trembling despite a grip that was turning her fingers blue. She glanced at the gun sitting on the passenger seat and fought the primal urge to do what must be done. To see the surprise in his eyes as she took from him what he had taken from so many others, she was sure, would make all the pain go away. But she needed him, and hated herself for needing him.

He was parked in a green Eldorado. The car was his, purchased with cash in early October. His mood matched the trace of disappointment in his eyes as he looked on. It was true things hadn't gone well for Scott after the Agency and that things had turned from bad to worse when Scott separated from Cynthia three months ago, but to find the Agency's former top operative sitting alone and drunk on a park bench at 4 a.m. seemed unreal, almost surreal. He had plans for Scott Evers, and none of them included returning him to the fold.

The two onlookers stepped out of their cars at almost the same time. Their thoughts and eyes focused on Scott alone. She touched a hand to the pins holding her wig, snatched the gun up from the passenger seat and then hurried off. He paused to look into the side mirror, straightening his tie and making sure hair was covering the growing bald spot in the middle of his head. A large manila envelope was on the Eldorado's passenger seat. Remembering the envelope, he opened the driver-side door and grabbed it.

Scott twisted the cap off the bottle, the already-broken seal allowing it to slip off all too easily and making it all too easy to raise the bottle to his lips. He squeezed his eyes together as the first rush of sweet and tangy raced across his tongue. Right then he wished he hadn't replaced the whisky with apple juice, but as the whiskey had already been spilled into the gutter, there was nothing he could do. As he put the bottle down, he glanced from the device in his hand to the tiny red glow coming from the left inside pocket of his sport coat. He twisted a nearly invisible earpiece farther into his ear and waited.

With business commuters already beginning their morning treks into the heart of D.C., the wait wasn't long. The device stopped at 802.315 megahertz. The unique digital signal code from cellular number 545-8992 as it fed into the cell net was decrypted and stored digitally in the device. A few seconds later, Scott received identity confirmation: Howard Allen Smith Sr. Shortly afterward the user ID was stored securely. From there, Scott connected to the wireless organizer in Mr. Smith's coat pocket. The organizer feed was slow but fast enough to snatch Mr. Smith's e-business card and other useful information before the car was out of range.

Scott took a rubber-tipped pen out of his right pocket and wrote into a palm-sized electronic notepad:

Howard Allen Smith Sr.

PR Rep.

5-star

Scott fancied himself the Grinch just then, but he wasn't

stealing Christmas. He was stealing lives. He stole lives to get back his own. The cell call was from a woman and although her voice was in his ear less than a minute before the device started searching again, it was enough to propel Scott's thoughts to Cynthia. Cynthia, who was waiting for him, for good news, and for the light at the end of the tunnel he promised her was there if only she would be patient a little longer.

Cynthia. Beautiful Cynthia, full of life at twenty-three, married to a man fifteen years her senior. A worn-out husk of what was once a strong man. A man who at twenty-three would never have let anyone get the best of him. He told her he'd come back for her when it was safe. That was three months ago and there was even more danger now.

As if coerced, Scott's gaze shifted to the front page of the *Washington Post*, which was on the bench beside him. A single article occupied most of the front page and just as the article's headline stated, the whole of the world had stopped yesterday. The president's statement on national television calling the shutdown of global financial networks and the National Federal Reserve System "a glitch, a coincidence and nothing to worry about," couldn't have been further from the truth. The outage started with the FTSE in London, spread to the CAC in France, the DAX in Germany then hit every major exchange in Europe. When the U.S. markets opened shortly afterward, the same thing happened on the NASDAQ, the NYSE and elsewhere.

Quotes in the article were a testament that there were some in Washington who understood there was a problem, but Scott had read the article and knew very few truly understood. The cascade effect wasn't an accident caused by the original London exchange outage. It wasn't a programming error either.

Billions were lost as a result of the outages. But Scott knew the shutdown wasn't about money. It was about control. Scott knew this if no one else did. It was all about information and its control.

Scott heard footsteps but didn't look up. An hour ago he had wondered if today was the day his shadow would step out of the car and approach him. Now he wondered if today was the day he'd be forced to put a bullet in the back of the other's head.

"I have something for you," a woman whispered, her voice calm.

Scott looked up. His eyes widened but the years spent in hellholes where his life depended on being calm and cool served him well. The device had told him about the woman parked in the Intrepid. He had marked her as a nonthreat, an obvious misjudgment. He said quietly as he raised the bottle to his lips, "Keep walking. There's a dangerous man coming up from the west end of the park."

The woman didn't move.

Scott guessed from the position of her hand in her pocket that she was holding a gun. He knew she had been following him since Monday and while he had given her two opportunities to confront him, she hadn't. He stood awkwardly, the bottle in his right hand swaying mightily as he staggered toward her and offered her a drink. Then with catlike quickness he leaned forward, reached his left hand into her right pocket and laid his index finger over hers on the trigger.

He whispered in her ear, "Scream while you're running away or he'll kill you."

The woman stared back at him. Her eyes empty and cold. It was a look Scott had seen many times in the mirror, and seeing it in her eyes affected him more than when he saw it reflected in his own. When the woman saw that Scott understood, she screamed and ran. But she didn't run because he wanted her to, she ran because it seemed the right thing to do. The look in her eyes haunted Scott as the echo of footsteps steadily approached from the west end of the park.

"Always were a real charmer," the other said as he stopped just within the yellow glow of the lamppost.

"Faith Presbyterian, come to save the drunken sinner," Scott said quickly. "Why today, Glen?"

"We need to talk, but not here and not in the open. Come with me to the Fredericksburg branch office."

Scott stared back blankly. "The pieces won't just glue back together."

"You're very wrong. They do."

Unmoving, Scott replied, "He was dead when I arrived in Munich. The rendition failed."

"You want to set the record straight. I'll help you. We'll take my car."

Scott slipped the device he had been hiding deeper into his pocket and then said, "I don't have the records."

The other smiled, the wolf showing his pearly whites. He didn't say what he wanted to. The plan was for the conversation to be as brief as possible to accomplish the job. He said what he had been saving, "Cynthia's ultrasound looked good. She told me she wants you to come home."

Scott scratched at the stubble on his chin. He wanted to grab the man about the shoulders and shake him like a rag doll. Instead he looked on, waiting for the next move. "Lousy disguise," Scott said finally to end the silence.

"Took you long enough."

"Bald and fat, cute. But don't mistake me for the gutter drunk I appear to be. I made you two weeks ago."

"The eyes—"

"—never lie," Scott finished.

"They don't, do they? But the woman still surprised you. Interested to know who she is and why she wants to kill you?"

"Not the first. Won't be the last," Scott shot back.

Glen handed Scott the envelope containing the ultrasound printout. He said, "If you come in, I'll call off the watchdogs. You can go home to Cynthia like I know you want to."

Scott reached out his hand to Glen's. "Is that a promise?"

"Scott, the rules have changed," Glen said, knowing the gesture had come too quickly to be sincere. "The Cold War is long gone but in its place we have a connected world. To survive you must play by the new rules. Can you agree to see things my way on this?"

Scott replied with a question. "What are you saying to me?"

"Why do you make everything so difficult? You know what I'm saying."

"Spell it out for me."

"Scott," Glen said, "I know what you're thinking. Even if you get by me, you won't make it out of the park. I have full authorization to minimize risks. You are about to become a risk. Do we understand each other?"

"You'd kill me?"

Glen snapped his fingers. "Just like that. Consider it an expedient debriefing."

Faster than the eye could follow, Scott drew a pen gun from his belt and pressed the tiny muzzle against Glen's jugular vein.

"Mistake number one," Glen said. "You're a damnable creature of habit. You come back to the states and lose the edge that kept you alive for the past 20 years in places I wouldn't have wanted to be in."

Scott pressed the gun harder against Glen's throat. "So this is going to turn into a lecture now?"

Glen leaned forward, unafraid. "How is Cynthia, by the way? Any problems? Pregnancy can go wrong in so many ways. You on the outside and every minute under the microscope of the recovery team isn't helping."

"Leave Cynthia out of this."

"Let's be sensible and discuss this like adults. You know it didn't have to be this way. You made it this way. Put the weapon away and come with me to Fredericksburg."

Scott lowered the gun. Glen took it, putting it in the pocket of his overcoat. The two went to his car. Glen drove. They arrived at the branch office a little after 7 a.m. By 9 a.m., Glen had completed the briefing and Scott was earnestly reviewing the mission dossier.

Glen watched, making sure his face didn't show displeasure. Things had gone much as he had hoped; still he had been so careful. A kinship slowly cultivated over the years, all building up to a single moment of truth—the choice that would change his life and Scott's forever. But Scott was making this a little too easy. Why?

Scott tossed the dossier onto the desk and looked Glen in the eye. He was silent for a time then said firmly, "You have hundreds of pages of nothing."

Glen smiled at the show of emotion in Scott's voice and eyes. Scott's real problem was that after 20 years he still felt everything. Glen cleared his throat. "A two-year official investigation. What did you think we'd turn up staying within the lines? We don't have that problem anymore. Do we? Five people know what we're discussing, and you and I are among them."

Scott said nothing. He stared at the photograph projected on the canvas behind Glen, knowing his eyes betrayed disbelief. He leaned forward. "John Ellis Wellmen is the richest man in the world. You can't be serious. Why do you want him?"

Glen Hastings emerged from the folds of the black leather chair. His dark brows bunched together. The heavy brown eyes beneath stared across the long mahogany desk that divided the room. "Extremely serious."

"His annual income is more than the G.N.P. of some entire nations."

Glen gave no indication that he hadn't known this.

Scott shifted uneasily in the chair and added quickly, "I'm not talking tiny, obscure third world either."

"There it is, in a nutshell," Glen shot back.

Scott's eyes went to the dossier on the desk, but he said nothing.

"Good," Glen said. He unlocked the briefcase, which had been on the desk, and put the folder into it. "His daughter's wedding is in the last week of January: Private, secluded, tropical. He'll be there for an entire week. That'll be your one chance."

"To hit the ranch?"

Glen glared across the open briefcase. "Security better than the Gray Room in Moscow at the height of the Cold War. We had someone on the inside for six months and got nothing."

"*Had?*"

"Wellmen can't possibly leave behind his business affairs for an entire week. He likes to keep a finger on every penny. To be sure, he'll have everything he needs to conduct business with him, computerized files, transaction records, you name it—all encrypted in his digital wallet and everything in his coat pocket right where you like it. There'll be hundreds of guests. Security will be limited. You'll have free reign."

"How much encrypted data are we talking about?" Scott shifted uneasily in his chair. "I thought if I came here you'd give me an out. Maybe a quiet position here in D.C."

"A position on the Council? I tell you what. I'll make you the Chairman, put your picture in the *Washington Post* and see how long it takes before they're sponging what's left of you off the seat of your car." Glen sank back into the folds of the black leather chair. "Sound good?"

Scott stood. "How much data are we talking?"

"A few hundred."

"Megabytes?"

"Gigabytes."

Scott threw up his hands. "If I touch this one… Hell, even if I could, what would you get out of it other than aggravation?"

Glen put down the slide projector's remote. "I know you've been following the headlines. Either you are on one side of this equation or the other. I have to know right now. I'm prepared to do whatever's necessary to get you back on our side. You and Cynthia want to make a life for yourselves. Take this assignment and afterward slip into an early retirement. I'll help you disappear if you need to."

"Disappearing's the easy part." Scott leaned on the desk, his right hand clenched in a fist. "Staying a ghost is the hard part."

Glen gestured for Scott to sit. "For Cynthia's sake," he said.

Scott hesitated, but did sit. "You know I don't do this sort of thing."

"Oh, please. I recruited you. You can do better than that." Glen picked up the remote and clicked it. The screen blanked for a moment, then a picture of John Wellmen and his family appeared. "Taken ten years ago, before the accident in California. His second wife, Katrina, and two sons, Mark and Kevin, are on his right. The girl on his left is his daughter, Jessica, from his first marriage. Sixteen in this picture."

"Sixteen?" Scott stared at the picture. He recognized those eyes. Eyes like those on a child's face cut into him even more than they had before. "Wait a minute…"

Glen clicked the remote again. "Taken at the funeral, five years ago. The last time Wellmen was seen in public. He lost his wife and sons to a drive-by shooter. The woman in the veil is Jessica. Twenty-one. The man on his right is his personal assistant, Kim Dong Gi. They call him Mr. Kim. He handles all contacts with the outside world."

Scott cut in, "Tell me right now if Wellmen is on the List. You and I both know the only way we'll ever get him is to kill him. I'm not one of your assassins."

Glen pursed his lips, his nostrils flared. He said calmly,

"That's why you're perfect for this job. Let's not forget about the one you did take."

Scott whispered, "I should have put a bullet in you while I had the chance."

"This is business, purely business. Even if you had killed me, you never would have gotten away. Use that brain of yours on occasion. At this point, I'm the only one between them and you." Glen broke off momentarily, regained his composure. "We have the dates narrowed to a seven-day window. Wellmen booked hotel reservations solid for weeks throughout the islands. Fortunately he could only get helicopter and airline reservations booked solid for that week."

"Doesn't want any unexpected visitors dropping in?"

"Relax," Glen said. "We want you inside his security. We want his data. Everything's in that digital wallet and he carries it on his person at all times. He even sleeps with the damn thing. He hates television cameras, outsiders, the public's prying eye. He's always careful, always. Even at the ranch you can't get within fifty yards of him without a strip search and his guards carry signal sniffers—top-of-the-line stuff stolen straight from us."

"And the wedding. Why at the end of January when Valentine's Day is only two weeks away?"

"You'd have to ask the bride that one."

"More like the bride's father. Do you think it's a cover for something else?"

"Doubtful. His one weakness is that he loves Jessica deeply, despite herself. He wouldn't do anything to spoil her big day."

"And the reservations?"

"Getting the reservations wasn't that difficult. I'm not just talking about money."

"Yeah, yeah. He owns a healthy number of hotels and has substantial influence in the U.S. tourist industry as a whole."

"In the dossier, wasn't it?" Glen glanced into the briefcase, then closed and locked it. "What you won't find in the dossier is the work some associates did on the Apollo reservation system to ensure that seven-day window."

"Why at the wedding?"

"Didn't read too close, or did you—no, you didn't forget, did you? All right, I'll say it. It's the only opportunity we'll have to find him in the company of more than two or three other people. The only time you'll be able to get close enough to him."

"I thought you wanted me in his data, not in his face."

Glen grinned, the wolf showing his pearly whites. "Come with me to Meade tomorrow. If things work out, you'll be on a plane Wednesday."

"I'll drive myself. If I see one of your suits within fifty yards, I'm gone."

"One o'clock sharp." Glen stood. It was a dismissal. Glen was sure Scott knew it, but Scott didn't move.

"There's one thing I have to know," Scott said. "Did your people have anything to do with the accident in California?"

Glen stood and walked Scott to the door. "Of course not. No family under the old rules."

Scott raised an eyebrow. "An accident?"

"Wrong place, wrong time." Glen opened the door and ushered Scott into the hall. "See you at one. Go home. I told Cynthia you'd be home for dinner."

"Stay out of my life!"

Glen shot back, "I am your life."

The slide projector was still on. Scott stared up at the picture of the funeral projected on the canvas behind Glen and couldn't help but wonder how far off his was. He turned away quickly, knowing he'd go to the meeting but not home.

Three months of separation couldn't fall away in an instant. If he cared, Glen or someone else would find a way to use that against him. Cynthia and the baby were safe as long as he kept his distance. For now they were the daughter and grandchild of the Chairman, and not the wife and baby of Scott Madison Evers.

Chapter 2

Ft. Meade, Maryland
Tuesday, 28 December

The Cold War had been over for more than twenty years and the Agency's centerpiece was proof positive that the spoils of war do not always go to the victors. The building was still monolithic. You couldn't shrink buildings, only budgets. The security that had always been omnipresent hadn't changed and the reason was the growing interest in domestic affairs.

Scott touched his badge to the elevator's reader. The doors opened and he stepped into the hall. He paused for a moment to look at the H-level directory and then hurried off in the direction of Conference Suite 18. He traversed the half mile of corridors in less than five minutes. The halls were empty, as were most of the offices.

He touched his badge to the room's reader, ignoring the thumb scanner, and watched for the reader's light to turn from red to green. He paused for a moment to catch his breath, tucked in his cotton shirt, put on the tan jacket, fixed his tie and then stepped into the room.

Glen was waiting for him. He escorted Scott into 18-C, pausing outside the closed door. "You're more than an hour late. The Chairman had another meeting, so we went ahead without you. It's just you and me now." Glen added softly, "You let me down."

"There was a mix-up upstairs."

Glen gripped Scott's shoulder from behind. He didn't say that he had arranged the mix-up; instead he indicated that Scott should open the door. Scott flashed his badge at the card reader. The light turned from red to green. Scott opened the door.

From behind him, Glen said, "As you can see, I got left with this entire mess."

Scott didn't say a word as he turned on the light. He just stared at the empty room.

Glen acted as if he remembered something and then said, "We're supposed to be in 18-A." He then led Scott down a side corridor to a different conference room. Inside, they found a conference table littered with digital recording discs. "I want you to go through the surveillance recordings of the Colorado ranch. Video first. Audio last. I'm going to sort out the paperwork and get rid of the duplicates. Let me know if the sanitizer bothers you."

Scott composed himself and left thoughts of Cynthia and the baby behind. "Is there anything in particular I'm supposed to be looking for?"

Glen smiled, apparently pleased. "You'll know if you find anything. I trust your instinct more than anyone else's analysis."

Glen turned on the sanitizer and started pulling discs out of their cases. He would sanitize most of the records to erase their contents permanently.

Scott turned to the surveillance recordings. He grabbed a stack of recordings and headed to the opposite side of the room, where racks of electronic equipment were set up for playback. The standard-issue surveillance equipment wasn't new to Scott. He powered up the computer, inserted one of the discs and waited for the system to finish initializing.

Sixty seconds later, he pressed Play and Search Forward. Everything on the recording for the first few hours was night vision green. Just before dawn flashed by, he saw something. He reversed the video and went through a frame at a time. He saw the front door open as three individuals emerged from the house. They shook hands with someone he couldn't see, then got into a truck and drove away. He noted the date and time, then pressed Play and Search Forward. He watched a mail truck come and go, a delivery truck, then the recording ended. He took the disc out and stuck in another.

It was nearly 9 p.m. when Scott removed the last disc and turned bleary eyes about the room to find Glen was gone. He rubbed his eyes with the heels of his hands and then eased out of the chair. A note on the table next to the stack of recordings read:

> *Be back in a few hours.*
> *I'll bring chow.*

Scott shook his head, stretched and then started on the audio-only recordings. He glanced at the disc label as he put on a headset. After making sure the foot controls were within reach, he began to search.

His thoughts wandered. Occasionally, he saw Cynthia's brown eyes in the back of his mind, but adrenaline kept sleep away. Glen wouldn't try to kill him here. Scott was sure of this. Somehow there was a place for Scott in Glen's twisted plan—at least for now.

Around 3 a.m. Glen returned. They ate, didn't say much. Afterward Glen went back to the data files and Scott went back to the recordings.

By 7 a.m., Scott was poring over the audio recordings again, putting the pieces together. A pad of paper beside him was marked up with a myriad of notes, things scratched out, circled, written over. Scott pushed pause, noted the time of the recording as 03:58:00.

Glen was still reviewing data files. "Useless, all useless," he was muttering to himself.

Shortly after 9 a.m., Scott called Glen over and pointed to the monitor. "Every Friday night coming. Every Monday morning leaving. I've seen their faces before in the *Wall Street Journal,* but their names weren't in the caption and the article didn't catch my eye. Senior partners in some big law firm in New York City. I've also got four interesting phone calls to a 212 area code. Not much content, but when you put the time of the calls together with their departure and then patch in the sixth line. Well, listen for yourself."

Glen put on a headset.

"Two separately dialed phone calls. The first is from New York to the ranch. I'm running the playback simultaneously. Channel one is in your right ear. Channel two, in your left ear. I'll start the video and audio at 03:52:30."

Glen bunched up his eyebrows but didn't say anything. Scott let the recordings run until the timer turned over to 03:58:00.

Glen looked puzzled. Scott ran the recordings back and played them again. "Close your eyes. Just listen this time. Wait till you hear the door opening, then look at the video."

Scott watched for Glen's eyes to widen and revelation to follow, but that didn't happen. Scott ran the video forward three frames, paused it. "There, do you see what he's putting into his pocket?"

Glen squinted. "A portable phone. So what?"

"Now what if I told you the disguised voice on the phone was John Wellmen?"

"You said the call was from New York."

"It is."

"John Wellmen was in New York?" Glen jumped to his feet. "You can't be serious. He hasn't left the ranch in months."

"No," Scott said tersely, "You're not following me." Scott adjusted the rate and pitch of the incoming New York call to reduce the effects of descrambling and then played the calls again. "Outgoing line three patched together with outgoing line six in New York. Maybe relayed somewhere. Maybe not."

"You lost me."

"Both calls are outgoing calls. Neither is incoming. That's what raised my suspicions. We're supposed to think that one line is incoming and the other is outgoing, but these are just decoys. The real conversation is happening on a different frequency and there's a link to a third party on a conference call that we're missing altogether."

"Are you saying the signals are multiplexed?" Glen understood the concept of stacking frequencies and transmitting them together. The Soviets had long used this tactic in the field to divide up the frequency spectrum and make signals more difficult to collect.

Scott started tapping at the keys on the computer's keyboard. "In a way. There's a subcarrier mixed in with the signal. It's carrying the actual conversation but is also using time division multiplexing. We don't have the equipment here to unravel it, but there is good news."

Glen nodded. Scott handed Glen a headset.

Scott said, "Listen in the silence. You can hear a warble in the background that sounds deceptively like a descramble echo, but it's not."

Scott stopped. Glen waited. "Damn it, Scott. I don't have the patience."

"Well, screw you!" Scott threw down the headset. "If I'm going to play your game, you can at least—"

"Whatever you might think, Scott, this isn't a game. I told you the rules have changed. We're playing for keeps. Winner takes all."

Scott took a swipe at Glen. Glen bobbed away. "You bastard. Put a bullet in my head now and save yourself the trouble later."

Glen bobbed away again, a little too slow. Scott's jab caught him in the mouth. "Now that's the Scott Evers I know. Quick of tongue, hand and eye. Almost makes me think of the early days."

Scott backed away, put his hands down. "I was eighteen. I didn't know what I was getting myself into then."

"You could've been the best. I saw it then."

"I am the best."

"Prove it."

Scott picked up the headset, nodded to the recorder, pressed Play. "It's the missing link in the conference call, scrambled using different encoding sets from the outgoing lines. It doesn't use TDM."

Scott played the recording again, descrambling the background voice. Glen listened. The voice said, "What about the engineer?"

There was an inaudible reply.

"I don't trust her. What about the Florida office? Has it been searched?"

A warble.

"The change affects nothing. I want it. Is that simple enough for you?"

A warble.

The line went dead. Glen asked, "Are there more conversations like this?"

Scott tore off a sheet of paper from the notepad, handed it to Glen. "The times and dates. Can we send this stuff to Analysis?"

Glen put his hand on Scott's shoulder. "I'll handle it. Go home to Cynthia. Get some rest. I already booked you on tonight's red-eye to Denver."

Scott wasn't going home but he didn't say this. Instead, he asked, "Tonight?"

"You'll be traveling as Randall Benton. You're a real estate attorney, looking to buy acreage for a resort. Everything else you may need is in the cover detail." Glen took an envelope out of an inside jacket pocket and stuck it into Scott's hand. "I want you to poke around and see what you can come up with out there. Nick from the Denver office will meet you at the airport. He's authorized to get you anything you need. This is need-to-know only and he's outside the loop. Don't tell him where you're going or what you are doing. Don't let him tag along. If he asks you anything, anything at all, direct him to me. While you're there, the only authorities higher than you are me and God. Do we understand each other?"

Scott didn't want to, but he did.

Glen looked at his watch. It was 12:45 p.m. "I have a 1 p.m. briefing that I can't miss. ... During this mission, there is no problem one phone call to me won't fix. When the results come back from Analysis, I'll call you. I want daily updates. Ops Out, Feet Wet procedures. Otherwise, I'll see you in a week or so."

It was a dismissal. Scott didn't move.

Glen seemed pleased and turned to an image frozen on the computer's second monitor. "If I had told you right from the start that those three gentlemen were, from left to right, Whuthers, Wolcott, and Williams, attorneys at law, would you have kept digging all night long through the recordings trying to find out their identity and in the process made a connection no one else made? Scott, I know you better than you know yourself. You work best functioning near zero. I want you in Denver hungry. If there's something to find, you'll find it. I'm counting on it. I'm your friend, Scott. You can count on that as well."

As Scott left the room, Glen looked at his watch. At 12:55 p.m., he closed the door, locked it from the inside, and then sat down at the table. Quickly he unbuckled his belt, slid it out of the loops of his pants, and then carefully detached the buckle. He untied his shoes, unstrung the laces partway, and then removed the shoes. He pried the gun barrel from the inside of the left shoe, the silencer from the right. A moment later he fit the barrel onto the top of the buckle, then attached the silencer. Afterward, he relaced his shoes.

He stood, relooped his belt. He concealed the gun, stepping out of the room. He looked around the side corridor. It was empty. He made his way to the rear door of Conference Room 18-C. The door was still slightly ajar, just as he left it. He opened it, removing the wad of putty as he went in.

An oaken table dominated the plain rectangular room. Glen crossed to it, noting that the Chairman was seated at the head position and the team code-named the Wellmen Four had already arrived. The Chairman set his glass of water down, cleared his throat, and then stood to shake Glen's hand. "We've already started, but that's all right. I'll introduce you and go on."

"No need for introductions," Glen said, "I know almost everyone here. John, Tom and Sarah were part of a Humint team I headed up in the Middle East. We spent three years together." Glen nodded to John and Tom. Sarah, who looked as radiant as ever, wouldn't look at him. "And I've seen the newbie around a few times."

The Chairman smiled. "Well, you won't need me anymore

then." He motioned to Sarah at the far end of the table. "Sarah," he said, "the show's yours again."

"You're not leaving, are you?" she asked.

"I'm afraid I must. Glen's the one who needs to know the facts. He's my proxy. Fill him in on everything."

Glen shook the Chairman's hand. "Thank you. I'll do my best, sir."

"I'm counting on it," the Chairman said as he departed.

Sarah handed Glen a folder without looking him in the eye, then turned back to the rest of the team. "As I was about to say, although our investigation showed there is inconclusive evidence against John Wellmen at this time, it did reveal some items of interest." Sarah touched a remote pad in front of her. The lights dimmed and a slide projector turned on. "This photo was taken a little over a week ago at the Colorado ranch."

Sarah clicked the remote again. "In fact, every Monday morning since March 2nd, you'll find these three individuals leaving the Wellmen's ranch at 4 a.m." She paused, tapped the projection screen with a pointer. "Here I've enlarged the frame to show the faces. From left to right, they are Whuthers, Wolcott and Williams. Now here's the billion-dollar question: Why are the three highest-paid lawyers in the free world spending every weekend at the ranch?"

Sarah paused to turn the lights back to full and to look Glen directly in the eye. "I think it's just cause to continue our preliminary investigation. I think we can get another six months with this. Hell, I know we can. They arrive by private jet, only at night, leave early when it's still dark, and never go outside the whole time they are there. Something's going on."

Glen turned to Sarah. "All the same, you did turn in your files and everything else for this case, didn't you? You know it's my ass now if you didn't."

Sarah shot back at him, "Everything's where it's supposed to be. Don't screw with my data system. We didn't miss a damn thing. Grant the extension and disposition your ass!"

Glen winked at her and decided right then, he wouldn't miss her at all. Before he hadn't been sure, but now he was. She would be the last, he told himself.

"What about the voice and data taps?"

Sarah turned to John. He was the wire man, always. John said, "I wish I could say otherwise, but I didn't find anything new."

"Who had wireless?"

The newbie said, "Me, sir. Todd Banovich."

"Any success in the descrambling effort?"

"His system is the best I've ever seen. I've cracked codes before, but this is something else. All incoming and outgoing wireless is scrambled using keys I've never seen anywhere else. Six months wasn't enough time."

Glen eyed Tom. "You were on the inside. Don't tell me you don't know anything new."

Tom shrugged. "I never got close enough. Wellmen never lets any of the staff into his level of the ranch. Mr. Kim handles everything down there."

Glen tossed a manila envelope onto the table, and then walked around the table until he was standing behind Tom. He put his hands on Tom's shoulders. "You know, in our line of work it's not entirely uncommon to have a secret bank account hidden away somewhere for a rainy day. You never know when it'll come in handy to make a quick getaway. But Tom here has an account with a hundred million dollars in it."

Tom tried to jump out of the chair. Glen held him in it. "Tell me," Glen whispered into Tom's ear, "Did you not find anything because you couldn't or because you were paid not to?"

Glen didn't wait for an answer. Blood was racing in his ears. The hand of God was on his shoulder. He shot Tom in the back of the head without a second thought.

The room became so quiet that to Glen it seemed he could hear the tension rippling in the air. He wiped the blood spatter from his cheek with a handkerchief from his pocket. He imagined the thoughts racing through their minds. He knew they were afraid to say a word, John especially. He'd been there before when things had gone sour. Human Intelligence wasn't work for someone with a weak stomach.

Glen walked over to Todd. Todd was shaking violently. "What's the matter, Todd? Worried? Your guilty conscience eating at you?"

Todd started whimpering. Glen was sure the newbie had just shit his pants. The smell was stomach-churning.

"Two bad eggs out of four. Dirty shame." Glen stuck the muzzle of the gun against the back of Todd's head and pulled the trigger despite Todd's shrill pleas.

Sarah shouted, "I don't want any part in this. I'm out!"

At the same time, John jumped out of his chair, put his hands up defensively. "I didn't take a bribe! If you're going to kill me, you're going to have to work for it."

Glen changed his mind about shooting Sarah last. "Okay," he

said, "you're out." He pointed the gun, one shot to the head. He never missed. Sarah never expected it. He could see it in her eyes. She still loved him and thought he loved her.

John ducked for cover, reached for his cell phone.

Glen walked around the table. "You should have taken the bribe. Janet would've made good use of the money."

John was screaming, "Hello, hello, hello!" into the cell phone but couldn't get a signal. As Glen came into range, John lunged from under the table.

Glen moved back to get out of the way, age robbing just enough of his speed so John's hands caught his legs. Smiling as he fell, Glen said, "You know, I'm screwing her. Janet's a real screamer."

John lunged, kicked. His face filled with rage and his foot came within an inch of Glen's head. Glen hesitated no more. He pulled the trigger, was surprised when the gun misfired and taken aback when John's next kick caught him in the side of the head.

As Glen got to his feet, John tackled him again.

"Who gave the order?" John shouted, his fists doing a one-two number on Glen's ribs.

Glen blocked but didn't go on the offensive. He'd been through worse. "It came from the top, John. It's only personal because of Janet. You should've been more careful and made more friends than enemies."

John didn't let up, his fists flying fast and frantic. "When I leave this room, I'm going to become a ghost."

"You're already walking dead. You just don't know it."

"Look who's talking." John grabbed Glen by the throat. "Very dramatic, I particularly liked the envelope. Tell me, what's in it?"

Glen choked out the words. "Yesterday's paper. I figured at least one in four of you had to be dirty."

"It's time to make amends, Glen. You ready to meet God?"

"God's already here with me. You just don't know he's on my side and not yours."

John shook his head and laughed. He held Glen with one hand while he untied and unlaced his boots with the other. Glen squirmed, tried to break free but couldn't. "Had these made special," he said as he bound Glen's wrists and ankles. "Struggle and you'll release the cyanide straight into your bloodstream. Don't struggle and your sweat will do the same in a few hours. Night, night."

Glen smiled. "Don't ever close your eyes, John. When you do, I'll be there. You can count on it."

Glen was about to say something else but everything became dark when John's fist connected with his skull. When he awoke sometime later with a pounding headache, he knew talk of cyanide was a bluff. He struggled then, squirming on the floor, knocking over a chair as he went. He was angry when he found he couldn't break free but he didn't give up.

There was a phone on the conference table. He grabbed the phone cord in his mouth and rolled until he heard the phone fall onto the floor. He rolled over to the phone; the receiver was off the hook. He looked for a way to dial.

He didn't see anything at first, but as he turned his head, he saw the pointer Sarah had used during the presentation. He struggled to get over to it, picked it up with his teeth, rolled back over to the phone.

Holding the pointer in his mouth, he used it to dial security, shouting into the mouthpiece, "Red alert, agents down, shots fired! Conference Room 18-C. Hurry, this is not a drill!" Then he waited, satisfied, knowing things had turned out better than he had expected. John Tippton had done what he had hoped, and now he had his patsy. He'd get even in time, but for now he had other things to worry about.

Chapter 3

Baltimore, Maryland
Wednesday, 29 December

A ten-foot security wall surrounded the twelve-bedroom home that had been a wedding gift from Cynthia's father. Eighteen cameras scoured the yard from the oval driveway to the iron gates to the line of elms in the backyard. The household staff was small for the neighborhood—a chef, a butler who doubled as the chauffeur, and a maid. Scott was parked half a block away, his rental hidden in the shadows of an alleyway. If he leaned forward in the driver's seat, he could see the east wall of the house and in the opposite direction clear to the corner. His plan was simple. He'd wait until the night had gathered full. Sneak into the house so that no one saw him. He'd see, but not talk to, Cynthia for what could be the last time, and then drive to the airport.

Inside the house, Cynthia was slowly coming down the long spiral stairs from the second floor. She made her way to the den despite herself. Soon she imagined she could hear her voice reading the headlines from the *Washington Post*. Scott always used her voice to read the *Post*. If it were a Sunday he'd still be scanning the papers. "Catching up with the world," he called it. She called it a contemptible habit.

She'd bought him the computer last Christmas. It had lifetime NewsNet access and a remote viewer so he could "catch up with the world" from his easy chair. It had seemed such a deal. She had also hoped that he would no longer leave mountains of paper all over the den. But he preferred hard copy, had to have hard copy. The only thing he used the computer for was to read the headlines to him until he found an article he wanted, and then he would tell the computer to print it.

"Has to feel like a newspaper," Scott told her when she fussed at him. The newspaper was like the ritualistic Sunday dinners that always had to come from the outdoor grill. Routines. Order, clear and simple. But that was one of the reasons she loved him. With Scott, life was a clear path. He didn't play mind games with her. He loved her; he showed her every day—when he was there.

She paused to look at her hair in the mirror at the end of the hall. The phone rang.

"Scott," she called out, "you going to answer that?"

The butler, Edward, said, "Madam, I'll be happy to answer it."

Cynthia didn't say a word. Even without seeing Scott, she

knew he was looking at his watch.

"Stop," Scott would tell the computer, then he'd say to her, "After twelve already, I'm reading the *Post* now, almost finished. After that, I'll do whatever you want. I promise."

The phone rang again. Cynthia walked to the door of the den. Her face flushed. Her toes tingled. Her jaw quivered. She peered into the dark and silent room.

The computer started to answer the call. Cynthia ran to pick up the phone. "Hello… Daddy, where are you? I've been trying to reach you since Monday. I kept getting your answering service. They wouldn't even tell me where you were. I'm worried about Scott."

"It's not their job to know where I am," Mr. Simons said. "I was in New York, but I'm back home now. I didn't forget your mother's birthday, I sent flowers."

"But that isn't…" Cynthia began, planning to tell him what she was thinking. Then finally understanding what he was saying, she replied, "What do you mean you sent flowers? We always go together."

Mr. Simons replied, "I promise this won't happen next year."

She eased her way into Scott's computer chair. "Business?"

Mr. Simons said, "Pumpkin, you know nothing else would keep me away."

"I love Scott," she blurted out. For a long time afterward there was silence on the other end of the line. "Daddy, are you there?"

"Yes, pumpkin," Mr. Simons replied.

"I know you're being forced into retirement, but you still have some power connections, don't you?" She asked, her voice wavering at the last few words. "You're still the Chairman, right?"

"I've a few connections, yes."

"Scott and I want to make a life for ourselves." Her voice trembled and became very soft, "Daddy, I want Scott to live to see his son grow up."

"How is the baby doing? When was your last check-up?" Mr. Simons asked.

"Daddy, I want Scott to live to see his son being born," Cynthia repeated.

"Are you crying?" Mr. Simons asked. "Take a deep breath and tell me what's wrong. Whatever's wrong, daddy'll fix it. Something to do with Scott, is that it?"

"Daddy, can you come tomorrow?"

Silence on the other end of the phone greeted her for a moment, and then Mr. Simons said, "I've got an early flight tomorrow. I'll be back on Friday. I'll come straight from the airport."

A moment ago Cynthia hadn't been crying, but suddenly the weight of three months' worth of anxiety became more than she could hold up under. It was her trembling jaw that brought the first tear to her eye and once the first tear rolled down her cheek, the others came like water through an open spigot. She whispered, "Just come now."

It was an hour and forty-five minutes later that the black sedan made its way into the driveway. Scott watched its progress along the drive, a muscle above his right eye twitching irritably.

Cynthia came out onto the porch. In the soft white of the porch lights she had never looked so radiant. Scott's heart stopped as he glimpsed her. She was wearing a maternity dress. Her long brown hair was cast over her left shoulder. Her deep brown eyes showed clear disappointment. He noted the thick makeup around her eyes, the bright lipstick, and knew it was all meant to hide the fact she had been crying by diverting attention from the bags under her eyes. Janet, who was with Glen, would see through this in an instant. Glen wouldn't.

He'd heard of couples that could finish each other's sentences. Sometimes, Cynthia could start his. He imagined that if he walked through the gates right then, she'd greet him by saying, "Traffic was terrible." It would be a statement, not a question. She'd open her arms to embrace him. He knew she'd smell the alcohol on his clothes but choose not to say anything about it. But the booze was gone now, gone along with his career and maybe his life.

Hearing Glen's and Janet's footsteps, Scott lurched back to reality. He slipped further into the shadows of the bushes, knowing his plans for getting in and out of the house easily were gone. He held still and listened to the voices. Cynthia's voice in his ears was like a beautiful, sad song.

"For the baby," Glen said, handing a tiny outfit to Cynthia.

"I picked it out," Janet said, "I hope you like it."

Cynthia held the outfit up to the light. "It's pink?"

"Of course," Janet said. "What if the baby's not a boy? You have to have at least one outfit to take her home in."

Cynthia rubbed her belly. "He's a boy. I am sure. A mother knows."

"My purse," Janet said.

Following her cue, Glen said, "You two go inside. I'll be right there."

Janet put her arm in Cynthia's and escorted her into the house. Glen walked slowly to the car. He wanted to give them enough time to talk but not delay so long as to be obvious.

He was unlocking the passenger side door when he saw something in the shadows that caught his eye. On his hands and knees, Glen slithered to the bushes lining the front of the house, the sense of possible danger driving him faster than his age should have allowed. Glen grabbed the shadow with both hands and thrust it against the house. There was no astonishment in his eyes, only concern, as he recognized the operative he had sent after Scott. He demanded, "Where is he?"

"Somewhere here, I'm sure of it."

Scott said from behind Glen, "Somewhere closer than you think."

Glen spun around, his right hand grasping for Scott's throat as he swung around. He said clearly, as he tightened his grip, "You can't imagine how much is riding on this, Scott. You can't imagine… and you slinking around your house. Use the damned front door!"

"Going to strangle me now, is that it?" Scott shot back.

Glen stepped back, regained his composure. "Never let your guard down."

For a moment Scott was puzzled. Was Glen trying to warn him to watch his back, or show him who was in control? Then Scott said, "I didn't. Why was he following me? I thought we were on the same team."

"Your lead came through. He was trying to get a message to you. An American Airlines flight leaves at 10:45 p.m. for Miami, be on it. You're already ticketed, same cover story, just go to the departure gate. Call me when you get there. I'll give you the details then."

"Miami, what happened to Denver—and what the hell happened to you? You look like shit, Glen."

"Look who's talking." Glen dismissed the other agent with a wave of his hand. "The other guy's a lot worse off, trust me."

"I didn't doubt that. You're a bastard, you know that?"

"So you keep telling me," Glen said as he started back toward the front door. "Are you going to come in and at least say hello to your wife? She's very distraught."

"Must've got the divorce papers then," Scott said coolly. He started to walk back in the direction he had come from.

Glen grabbed Scott by the collar and spun him around. As he did so, he grabbed the younger man's hand, twisted and applied pressure, bringing him to his knees. "She's the only reason you're not six feet under. You don't divorce the Chairman's daughter."

Scott looked up, sure of himself. "Break the arm and I'll be pretty useless. You may as well handle this damn operation yourself."

"Scott, don't bite the hand that feeds you. He's the one who told us to bring you back into the fold. You owe him. You're going to do the right thing."

"The right thing is to stand up, put a bullet in your head and then one in mine."

"Always the charmer. Well, that charm is going to get you killed. You want your son to grow up without a father?"

Scott pretended that he didn't hear the voices earlier. "A boy, really?"

"To confirm there needs to be another reading but Cynthia

won't hear of it. She's certain it's a boy, doesn't care about the anomaly in the reading. That's good enough for me. If you talked to your wife, maybe you'd know that."

In the back of Scott's mind, there was joy but his face showed nothing. His only reaction was to break Glen's grip and stand. If he cared, they'd find a way to use that against him and then it wouldn't matter if Cynthia was the Chairman's daughter—or the President's daughter, for that matter.

Scott looked at his watch. "You said 10:45. I'd better be going. Security can be a nightmare, even with cleared passage."

Janet called out from the front porch, "Glen, you coming in?"

Scott could hear Cynthia's voice behind her.

"I think you have a few minutes," Glen said. "You weren't there for Christmas. It's almost New Year's for crumsakes. You have my word that Munich is forgotten. Officially, you've been classified as on mandatory paid-leave after being 'recovered' from hostile ops. Hell, the Chairman's even written you a citation."

"Citation?"

"It's in the car. That's what I was getting out of the car, a framed plaque and everything: Scott Madison Evers distinguished himself on December the 1st during the—"

Janet called out. "Are you boys ready?"

"Janet knows?"

"Janet knows and Cynthia has probably guessed by now what the big surprise is, so you can play this as the biggest ass in history or follow my lead." Glen stepped out of the shadows, moving to the sidewalk and the car. "On the way. Here comes the big surprise!"

Scott followed Glen, his eyes catching Cynthia's and his heart making his mind forget everything as he ran to the steps.

"The big surprise," he said as he wrapped his arms around her. "But I'm afraid it's out of the frying pan and into a—"

Cynthia touched a finger to his lips. "The baby's a boy," she whispered in his ear. "He's healthy and strong—a real kicker. He's been waiting for daddy to come home, and so have I."

Janet and Glen excused themselves. Scott and Cynthia barely noticed.

When the two finally decided to go into the house, Cynthia was the one who picked up the box from the steps. She opened it, admiring the plaque for a moment before she led Scott away. "Daddy really did come through," she whispered to herself. "I never should have doubted."

Chapter 4

Baltimore, Maryland
Thursday, 30 December

Cynthia lifted her head from the toilet, flushed and pulled herself to her feet. She turned on the shower, waited until the water was warm, removed her robe, and then stepped in. Another month, another week, another day, she told herself as she lathered up the soap and tried to let the warm water rinse away her disquietude. Her gynecologist told her the morning sickness would probably end with her first trimester—the doctor was wrong. Today was the beginning of her second trimester and she had expected the morning sickness to disappear almost magically—but it hadn't.

A few minutes later, she shut off the water. She dried herself with a towel. After clearing the steamy mirror, she stared at her reflection. Her breasts were starting to swell. They hurt. Everything hurt. Everything was swollen. Get it together kid, you're a mess… she told herself.

She took a deep breath. Someone knocked on the door. It was Edward. He said, "Mr. Simons is here, Miss Cynthia. Shall I tell him you are on your way down?"

She looked into the mirror. The hurt returned to her eyes. She put a hand to her mouth, closed her eyes and took a deep breath. She wasn't ready for this.

"Are you all right, Miss Cynthia?"

"Tell my father I just got out of the shower. I'll be down in a moment."

She put on a robe, wrapped her hair in a towel and then sat on the edge of the Jacuzzi tub until her knees stopped shaking. She walked slowly down the stairs. She knew her father would wait in the library—he preferred the library, said it was the only room in the house where he felt comfortable. More likely it was the only room in the house that wasn't bugged. She knew this— she wasn't as naïve as she pretended. The family "business" had taken her mother and she wasn't about to let it take Scott as well.

She paused in the hall to collect her thoughts and then entered. "Daddy, the flowers were beautiful, but they would have been even more beautiful if you had brought them yourself."

"Pumpkin, you look beautiful, healthy." He held out his arms.

She hesitated. The game, she reminded herself, it's all about following the rules of the game.

"Come here, tell daddy what's wrong and I'll fix it."

She still didn't move. "Was the business trip really that important? You couldn't have pushed it back a day? Mom would've been fifty. Fifty was special to her."

"Is that what this is all about? Why I drove all the way out from the airport through rush-hour traffic?"

"Yes—No, it's about Scott. He hasn't been himself lately. I'm worried about him."

"I'm sure it's nothing. Now, if you don't come over here and give me a hug, I'm going to put you over my knee." Cynthia smirked. They embraced. "Now, isn't that better?"

"Daddy, I know he's in trouble."

"Pumpkin, how do you know he's in trouble?"

She took a seat next to him, braced herself, told herself to be brave, to look daddy in the eye. "Glen was here Sunday."

"Glen who?"

"Glen Hastings," she snapped, hormones and morning sickness getting the better of her. "I know I shouldn't have listened in, but I had to try to find out what was wrong. I heard everything. Scott's in trouble, daddy. Do you think you could pull some strings and get him reassigned?"

James Simons, daddy to Cynthia, reached over and wiped the tears from her cheeks. "Pumpkin, I'm sure you're just upset, but I will see what I can do to help out." But in his eyes, she saw the Chairman and not her father. If there was one thing she had learned from Scott, it was how to read someone's eyes.

"Thank you." She kissed his cheek, trying to hide the sudden trembling of her jaw. She'd gone too far with her admission. She wasn't supposed to know anything and where before he had only absently listened to her, he was now paying full attention. "You know I really liked it better when he was just working with his gizmos. Now that he's working in negotiations it's just been a nightmare."

"Yes, negotiations can be tough," he said with a smile.

"Dangerous, more like. You didn't tell me."

"You have to understand, I didn't know the last assignment would—"

"Don't blame yourself. I don't think anyone could've guessed that it'd go on for so long, especially through the holidays. I'm just glad he was able to come home for a few hours before heading back. But I'm worried that the work is too dangerous. All it takes is one wacko with a gun and Scott—"

"Scott's a technical specialist, pumpkin. He's not supposed to be—"

"But he was."

"Well, this time, perhaps. I think it just happened because he has a common background. It's not everyday we crack one of these cybergang cases wide open, you know. He's a real—"

"Hero, yes I know: I read the plaque. But does it have to be Scott who—"

"I'm afraid it does. He's made a connection with their leader and now that they're talking, we need to find out everything we can."

She waved her hand at Edward. Edward set the tray on the table beside her. "Earl Grey?"

"Yes, ma'am. Strong, three-minute steep, just the way you like it. The biscotti are fresh, just baked."

Edward excused himself. Cynthia thanked him, then turned back to her father. "Tea? It's imported, some of the best." He nodded and she poured. She smacked his hand when he reached for the sugar. "No sugar. You don't need any of that."

Mr. Simons smiled, sincerely. "No, I don't. Your mother'd be laughing right now if she were here."

"She would, wouldn't she. Next year, we'll go together?"

"Yes, we will."

***

Scott unzipped the garment bag, put the suits into the motel closet, put the Beretta in the left boot and the Browning into the shoulder holster. He stretched out on the bed and propped his head against a pillow. He closed his eyes, but didn't sleep—wouldn't sleep. He left that part of him behind in Baltimore. The part of him that was here in a forty-dollar-a-day motel room in downtown Miami didn't need sleep to perform. Oh he'd sleep all right, an hour here, a few minutes there, but only when he couldn't go on otherwise.

Right now he was trying to sort out the cryptic message he'd received from Glen when he checked in. He saw the words in his mind's eye and tried to reorder them. He hated Caesar alphabet encoding and was sure that if anyone was watching, they would have sorted it out by now anyway.

He rummaged through the bedside nightstand. Finding a pad of paper and a pen, he wrote:

Friday, 2 p.m.

Jessica Wellmen

Southeast Financial Center

Not a team player

As he wrote, the videophone and the glossies under the plastic tabletop caught his eye. A caption under one of the pictures read: THE ONLY SAFE SEX IS PHONE SEX. FOR THE ULTIMATE, CALL SALT AND PEPPER. Scott chuckled for a moment. The phone book was under the videophone. He grabbed it and looked under the W's. What he found surprised him. There wasn't a listing for a Jessica Wellmen.

He looked for the Southeast Financial Center next, found a listing, but before he dialed their informational number, he blacked out the lens on the phone. "Yes, I'm trying to find someone who works... I should have called directory assistance? Will they be able to tell me... They won't? Thank you."

As he hung up the phone, he looked down at the tabletop. The ad for Sid's Pizza, printed in bold neon red, caught his eye: SID'S PIZZA 555-3758. DOWNTOWN, CHEAP, WE DELIVER. He called the number. A guy with the worst Italian accent he'd ever heard said, "Hold a minute, then I'll take your information."

He ordered a pizza with the works. Afterward, he drummed his fingers on the nightstand while he considered his next move, and that's when the light went on. He picked up the phone and dialed information.

The voice said, "What city please?"

"Miami."

"What listing?"

"Jessica Wellmen."

There was a moment of silence, then an operator said, "I've checked the listings, and there is no Jessica Wellmen."

"Can you check for the area?"

"Okay, sir… I'm checking for the big cities, Fort Lauderdale, Hialeah, Kendall, Sunrise, there's lots of Wellmen but no Jessica Wellmen. Do you know the street address?"

"Is there a way you could check outside the 305 area code?"

"I've already cross-referenced. No listing for a Jessica Wellmen, or even J. Wellmen, but I do have a J. Wellmen and Associates in Boca Raton."

He grinned. "What's the number?"

He hung up, then dialed the number.

A friendly-sounding woman answered the phone, "J. Wellmen and Associates. Can I help you?"

"Is Ms. Wellmen in?" Scott asked, switching on video receive. The woman also had a pleasant face. More importantly, with a red sweater draped over her shoulders and clad in a light pink blouse, she looked like a secretary.

"Gone for the day, down at the Symphonic. Her sister's the conductor you know."

"I was looking for Jessica, I believe. Well, actually, I'm not quite sure who I was looking for."

"We have three departments and fifteen consulting engineers."

"I think it was Jessica. Tall brunette, wears wire-rimmed glasses."

"I think you're mistaken. Jessica's been strawberry blonde long as I've known her."

"What was I thinking, long hair though and glasses, right?"

"No, no glasses. Doesn't even like to wear sunglasses. Why don't you just come down to the office, I'll find out which associate you spoke with and we can—"

"No, I'm sure it was Jessica. Will she be in tomorrow?"

"She'll be in Miami on business, but she'll be back Monday."

"Is she staying in Miami tonight?"

"Yes. Do you want to leave a message?"

"No, I'll call back on Monday." Scott hung up the phone and leaned back against the pillow. He could afford to sleep now that he didn't have to spend hours chasing around the Southeast Financial Center trying to find someone who wasn't even in Miami—yet. Some things were just too easy.

He was almost asleep when someone knocked on the door and yelled, "Sid's Pizza. Hurry, your pizza's burning my hand."

The instant his head left the pillow, Scott came fully alert. He took the gun from the holster and stuck it into the back of his pants. He opened the door with the chain in place—not that the chain would really stop anyone but because it would give him an extra instant of reaction time. "How much do I owe you?"

"Twenty-two fifty, plus tip."

Scott took twenty-five dollars out of his wallet, and then unchained the door. He glanced at the deliveryman's ball cap as he took the pizza. "Rainbows, local team?"

The guy looked at him strangely. "You could say that. Enjoy, *mahalo*."

He closed the door, set the pizza on the bed. He stared blankly at the wall while he tried to remember something, then it clicked. Rainbows—Hawaii. The last time he'd seen a Rainbows game it'd been... He tried to think—must've been...

He ate a slice, then pushed the pizza aside and lay down on the bed. He stared up at the ceiling. He remembered now and knew why he blocked the memory. His father had taken him to the games at Aloha Stadium during the year he'd been stationed in Hawaii and Scott had visited. Had it really been that long ago?

He pushed memories of the past out of his mind as he ate another slice of pizza. The past was a painful place. He drove out to the Southeast Financial Center around 10 a.m. on Friday morning. Not because it was a long drive from the motel or a hard place to find. He wanted to check the place out. He knew who to look for—a woman with long, strawberry blonde hair, no glasses and probably wearing slacks, somehow he couldn't picture Ms. Jessica Wellmen wearing a dress—and when to look for her, around two. But he didn't know who she was going to meet— would it be Whuthers, Wolcott or Williams, all three, or someone else entirely—or where they would meet.

He knew Jessica had come from Boca Raton the night before, but why? It was a mere forty-five minute drive to Miami—a few hours in rush hour, but they were meeting at two. Obviously she wanted to arrive fresh, and maybe she didn't want to worry about being late—or early. If that were the case, she'd come by cab, he knew it. He had only to pick the right vantage point to see her arrival.

As he walked around the financial center, he started thinking. Why Miami, why not just meet in Boca Raton? Why two o'clock? Why the Southeast Financial Center? It seemed the answer was so obvious that he was overlooking it because it had to be right there in front of him.

He stopped walking, looked at the people around him, then asked himself again. Why Miami, why not Boca Raton? Was it Miami International? But that wasn't enough, whoever Ms.

Wellmen was meeting could have caught a commuter flight to Boca Raton.

Crowds? Maybe.

Crowded—easy to blend in? Yes…

Why two o'clock? Was the answer the same? Everyone would be coming back from lunch—crowds.

Why the Southeast Financial Center? Any place in Miami during midday was crowded. Why here? Was there an office in the center Wellmen owned?

No, even if he owned the whole damned thing, that wasn't it. The point was that John Wellmen didn't own office space here, because if he did they would just conduct business in a private office somewhere and if they were going to do that, why not in Boca Raton? No, Jessica wasn't a team player. She was a wild card.

Scott thought back to the drive from the motel. What had he seen? What had he been looking for—a ninety-five-story building.

He chuckled. Suddenly, all the pieces fell into place. Whoever was coming didn't know Miami but knew how to find a tall building—just look up. But why come to a crowded place in a city you're not familiar with and to a place where you have no control?

He thought about this for a moment. The answer seemed suddenly clear, obvious—Ms. Wellmen wasn't just a wild card, she was holding the cards. She had something they wanted and she knew she was in control.

His question became: Was she in danger because of that and what would they do to get what they wanted?

Around quarter to two a taxicab pulled up to the curb. He looked on impatiently. Taxies had been coming and going all day and more so since noon. He saw high heels first, a flash of stockings, and as the woman moved away from the cab, black slacks, white blouse and a black business jacket. The woman was wearing sunglasses, and her brown hair was in a tight bun. He looked back down at the *Miami Herald*.

The front page was pretty grim:

CHILLED FINANCIAL MARKETS
FAIL TO WEATHER STORM:
CRISIS IN MAKING

But the accompanying article showed no one was really paying attention and the hustle and bustle at the Southeast Financial Center only backed this up. It was as if no one noticed that global financial networks were without a pulse during the outages—as if the financial storm would all blow over after the New Year. But he wasn't as optimistic as those around him. He remembered the crash of October 1987, the dizzying fall of September 2001, and everything that followed.

For fifteen seconds the world had been without a pulse. And in those few precious seconds, billions of dollars of market capitalization disappeared. Anyone playing heavy in the short end of the market came out richer. Anyone playing heavy in the long end of the market came out poorer. Couple the damage. Topple corporations. Make and unmake multibillionaires.

How do you attack democracy and win? How do you take control and keep it? How do you overcome immeasurable odds and survive? It wasn't by stockpiling nuclear weapons. It wasn't by dropping bombs. It wasn't through acts of terror. It was through the one thing that fuels economies and drives our world.

Even Fidel Castro's Cuba couldn't survive without it and this fact burns deep in hearts and minds. Marx had his communist doctrines, Lenin his socialist doctrines. Marxists and Leninists. Marxism-Leninism. Mao Tse-tung's China, Maoists. So many variations, all with the same fatal flaws. The fall of the U.S.S.R was only a precursor, the fall of the Berlin Wall only a symbol. The reality check: The greed and corruption that followed.

There was no maybe about it; there was only certainty. But he knew it wasn't just about the money. It was about control. Control the money by controlling the flow of information, by stopping global commerce and exchange. Everything was linked to the Munich assignment—the assignment he was the only one to come back from. But there were times when he thought it would have been better if he hadn't made it out alive.

He should've died with the rest of his team—the captain going down with the ship as it were. Captains who survived their crews when the ship went down weren't regarded well and in his circle, survival in those circumstances meant something else entirely.

The minutes ticked by. Another cab pulled up. Scott looked up momentarily. Just then someone said, "Excuse me?"

Scott didn't say anything. He was waiting for the cab's occupant to emerge.

The guy tapped him on the shoulder. "Eh buddy, you know what time is it?"

Scott didn't have to glance at his watch to know what time it was, but he did anyway. "Almost two."

"*Mahalo.*"

Scott folded the newspaper. The cab's occupant emerged, but it wasn't Jessica Wellmen. It was a man wearing a thousand-dollar suit, lugging a leather attaché case and staring up at the top of the financial center as if it were a monument. It was Whuthers of Whuthers, Wolcott and Williams. Whuthers went back to the taxi and asked the cabby something, then looked back up at the building. The cabby shook his head, waved his arm and pointed as he spoke, then Whuthers paid the cabby and the cab sped off.

Scott watched and waited. He took a pen out of his pocket and circled something in the want ads. As he stuck the pen back into his pocket, a loud bang sounded from across the street. The sound, not dissimilar to a car backfiring, didn't alarm anyone—except Scott. To his ears, the sound, muffled or not, echoed like a gunshot.

He looked around, tucked the paper under his arm, then started into the financial center. Whuthers made his way to the elevators. Scott followed, noticing how tight the lawyer's grip on the attaché case was. As Scott filed into the elevator, he pushed ninety-two after Whuthers pushed eighty-nine.

Before the doors closed, the press of the business crowd thrust Scott right up alongside the unsuspecting Whuthers. The ride toward the summit of the Southeast Financial Center went slowly. As the elevator emptied out, he nonchalantly shifted to the opposite side. Soon there were only the two of them and one gray-suited old man. When the doors opened for the 89th floor, he stepped expectantly forward, but Whuthers didn't move. He pretended to suddenly notice this wasn't the floor he wanted, and took a step back.

On the ninetieth floor, the old gentleman stepped out. The doors closed. Scott's mind started to work. He watched the lights above the elevator doors move: Ninety-one. Ninety-two. The elevator's buzzer rang. The doors opened. Scott hesitated, considered his options, then stepped into the hall. He glanced back over his shoulder. Whuthers was still leaning against the elevator wall. The elevator doors were almost closed.

Scott spun around, stuck his hand in between the closing doors. The doors jerked open. He jumped into the elevator.

Whuthers didn't move. He was wearing sunglasses, so Scott couldn't see his eyes. Scott glared at him.

Behind him, Scott heard the doors close. He spun around, hit the emergency stop button and drew his gun. He whirled back around to Whuthers, but Whuthers still didn't move. Scott shook his head in disbelief. He expected some response—*but no response?*

"The briefcase," he said almost cordially, "I'll take it now."

Whuthers' droopy scowl didn't change. Scott brandished the gun, then reaching out with the opposite hand, grabbed Whuthers' neck. There was a tightening in his gut as he realized he didn't feel a pulse.

In an instant, he knew he didn't have time to puzzle over a dead man—there was no way he was going to explain his presence at the crime scene to the Miami police department. He would restart the elevator and get out of the building as quickly as he could. And there was only one way to be sure, absolutely sure, that he got out of the building without being detained: Ride the elevator to the first floor and go out through the front entrance as if nothing had happened—because nothing had happened until someone else discovered it, then it was like Schrödinger's Cat.

Without hesitation, Scott pried the briefcase from Whuthers' hand, propped him back against the side wall, then started the elevator. The first time the doors opened on the thirty-second floor and someone stepped into the elevator, he braced himself for discovery, but nothing happened. No one screamed. No one even seemed to notice poor Mr. Whuthers. They were all too busy—probably looking forward to the end of a hectic week and the holiday. People got on and off the elevator at a number of floors, all the way down to the first floor where Scott got off and never looked back.

He walked at a leisurely pace to the parking garage, got into the rental car and drove off.

Hours later, he scratched at his right temple, rubbed sleep from his eyes with the heels of his hands. He peered out through stained curtains, momentary disbelief showing on his face at the arrival of a misty dawn.

Too many hours ago, he had checked in with Glen. He used the pay phone down the street and while he mostly used codes, he was still very careful about what he said. Glen's office phone was subject to monitoring at any time, and Glen could only ensure that outside parties weren't listening in.

Glen was careful too, his, "Are you off to Orlando tomorrow?" wasn't even in the book, but Scott understood what Glen meant just the same—what's the next move? Scott's next move was Jessica Wellmen. He wanted to drive out to Boca Raton right then, but Glen told him to check hotel registers first. The registers had been a waste of time.

For hours since, Scott walked in circles around the cramped motel room. Telling himself there was no way the attaché case had been empty when Whuthers entered the financial center. No way.

There had to have been a switch, a switch in the elevator, a switch he hadn't seen. So many people coming and going, and he hadn't watched the case. Stupidity, there was no other explanation, not lost youth, not the booze—he quit the booze—plain and pure stupidity, nothing else.

Out of the corner of his eye, he saw the flashing neon sign of the liquor store down the street. Any other time he would have wondered if it was still open, but not now, now he thought of Cynthia and her stupid sticky notes. Cynthia and the baby, who he must forget if he was ever going to get his head screwed on straight and think only about what he was supposed to be thinking about. He knew what he had to do. He took her picture out of his wallet and set it on the nightstand, intent on leaving it there.

He wanted to call her, and before he knew it, the dial tone was in his ear. But even his subconscious knew better than to place the call. He stuffed the picture into the trash, got out the Rand McNally road map of the state of Florida, and memorized the main streets of Boca Raton. The way he figured it, he could catch a catnap, check out, and be in Boca Raton before 10 a.m.

What a grand way to spend New Year's Day.

Chapter 5

Boca Raton, Florida
Sunday, 2 January

The wind shifted. The tiny sign over the door creaked. Scott turned up the collar on his waist-length tan jacket as the rain thrashing the concrete made its way into the shadowed doorway. He looked up and down the sleepy street, waited until he was sure no one was about, then slipped the picks into the lock. The lock opened easy, too easy, almost as if to invite him in. He looked over his shoulder, then slipped inside the offices of J. Wellmen & Associates.

He turned on the battery pack of the night vision goggles, slipped the goggles into place, and suddenly a world of greens unfolded before his eyes. The reception area was dingy and smaller than he imagined. There was a metal desk, a few chairs, an ugly couch, a coat and a plain wooden door leading to another room.

He went to the desk and examined the daily calendar. On Friday, December 3, there was a note jotted down about the Symphonic Pops. A name, Helen—*Jessica's sister?*

He tried to flip back through the pages but had to remove a glove to flip through the pages singly. Thursday: Nothing. Wednesday: Meet client 2:30. Tuesday: Lunch Helen 1:00. Monday: Nothing. He skipped forward and found three days were missing—Thursday, Friday and Saturday.

Next he rummaged through the desk drawers, didn't find anything unusual. He was about to see what was behind the door when he heard something outside: A noise, like someone tripping over a garbage can. He killed the power to the NVGs, waited.

Someone fiddled with the door handle. His thoughts began spinning. He had watched the place all through Saturday and well into Sunday. No one moved near the place then—why now, in the wee hours of a Sunday night?

His heart skipped as the door opened. He lifted his gun from its holster and shrank into a corner beside the couch. The wall gave way beside him, and he groped with his hand, discovering a paneled door leading to a closet he hadn't seen earlier. He slipped into the closet, just as the lights turned on.

He heard something slap the desk, a rattle of keys, a door closing. Someone in heels walked over to the couch. The heavy odor of a flowery perfume filtered under the closet door on a puff of air and behind it came the powerful scent of alcohol. He waited for a time, then cautiously slid the door open a fraction of an inch and stared into the brightness. His eyes adjusted and he saw a woman lying on the couch. The bottle of scotch she had been holding was spilling onto the floor.

He eased the closet door open and crept to the couch. The woman didn't move. It could have been the secretary he had talked to on the phone. The hair color was right, but he couldn't be certain. Her face was squashed against the canvas of the couch.

He opened the door that led from the reception area, expecting to find a hallway dotted with doors. Instead he found what appeared to be a single room. He saw no harm in turning on the light now and did so. In the far right corner, there was a small square section cut out of the room that he was sure led to a bathroom or closet. Against the near wall sat a small desk cluttered with wires, cables and small gadgets. Near the desk were racks of equipment. The floor was buried end to end in electronic gizmos, but there were no three departments, no fifteen desks for fifteen consulting engineers. One desk, for one lonely engineer.

The desk seemed a promising place to start. Scott picked his way across the floor to it. His eyes lit up when he saw a black leather attaché case sitting on the floor behind the desk. He set the case onto the desktop and opened it. Inside was a wig, a woman's wig with long brown hair. He made a toothy grin—at least he had been right about the slacks and the cab.

He rummaged through the desk, but didn't turn up anything useful—not even a date book or client list, which seemed strange. He glanced at the phone on the desk, a vintage rotary type, and noticed it had a different number from the one he called on Friday. He remembered the video phone on the front desk—it would have a programmed data list.

He went back to the reception area. The woman on the couch hadn't moved. He went to the phone, tried to access its database of phone numbers and found something he didn't like. It was erased clean. On a whim, he picked the phone up, got the dial tone, then held his breath as he pushed the redial button. A number started dialing out and feeding to the video screen. 1-4-1-0-5—suddenly something hard and cold was jammed into his other ear. A slurred voice said, "Drop the phone or I'll blow your head off."

He dropped the phone, started to turn around.

"Put up your hands, asshole." The woman started to frisk him with one hand. She found his holster. He let her take his gun. "Wouldn't you know it, another cop."

"I'm not a cop." He started to put his hands down.

The woman rammed the gun further into his ear. "Then who are you?"

"Take the gun away from my head, and maybe I'll tell you." The woman took a step back. Scott showed her his hands, made sure she understood they were empty, then slowly reached down to his boot. "Two fingers. I'm not going to try anything, so please don't shoot," he said as he lifted the gun from his boot and set it onto the desk. "If you're going to frisk someone, do it right."

The woman lowered the gun a bit and took another step backward. She wasn't very steady on her feet and the gun swayed all over the place.

"Look, if you point the gun away from me, we can talk. Or better yet, put it away." When she didn't, he shrugged and turned up his hands. "If I was going to hurt you, I would've. You were passed out on the couch, remember?"

She dropped her arm. Scott lurched forward and snatched the gun from her hand, sticking his thumb in front of the hammer as he did so. The woman started screaming and staggered backward. Scott released the hammer on the gun, set it onto the desk, then helped her over to the couch.

She eyeballed him, bewildered. "Trash can next to the desk. Bring it... I'm going to be sick."

He brought it.

He waited for the color to return to the woman's languid face. Good thing he had made coffee.

His watch said it was almost 6 a.m., but what little he could see of the street through a gap in the thick curtains was still dark and dreary. The rain hadn't stopped. It had been raining for hours, pounding and cleansing the concrete. "How's the coffee going down? Too strong, more cream?"

The woman shrank farther into the corner of the couch. It seemed the more sober she became, the more frightened she became. She drank the coffee almost reluctantly as if she didn't want the drunk to end. Scott could remember days like that—sometimes you didn't want to remember the things you'd done the night before.

She said, low yet firm, "Don't want to rob me, don't want to kill me, don't want to rape me—too old and ugly for you now, is that it?"

Scott noticed the youth hidden behind wrinkles and puffy blue eyes. "You're Helen?"

She relaxed a bit. "My body, not my brain, or is that vice versa." She frowned, put a hand to her forehead. "My head's going to kill me in the morning... I'm not a drunkard if that's what you're thinking."

"It is morning," he said quietly. "What time does the office open on Mondays?"

"Just who are you and what are you doing here?"

He said what was safest. "I'm conducting an investigation."

"On Jessica?"

"What makes you say that?"

"You're not the first. A P.I. was here a few weeks ago. My sister's not in any trouble, is she?"

He pointed to the red sweater on the coat rack. "Your receptionist, what's her name?"

"Give me a minute—No, there it is, May. May Parker... Wait, if you're following Jessica, you have to know where she is. We were supposed to meet last night, to celebrate."

"Her return from Miami?"

Helen frowned again. "No, my good fortune. Isn't that a laugh?... Aspirin, I need aspirins... No, better, I think I'm going to sleep."

"You need to walk around." Scott helped her stand. "Where are the aspirins?"

"Bathroom," Helen moaned. "But I don't think I'm ready to walk."

He put his arm around her to help steady her. She shrank away and stumbled back onto the couch. He brought her legs up onto the couch with the rest of her body, then put a cushion behind her head. "When was the last time you saw Jessica?"

She draped an arm over her eyes. "Thursday."

"Jessica didn't call you when she came back from Miami?"

She was silent.

"Helen, Helen?" He brought the sweater from the coat rack and wrapped it around her. He lifted her billfold from her purse while she was passed out. Not much to find: a driver's license and a credit card. Both belonging to Helen Johnson.

With his feet propped on a chair, he sat facing the front door for the next several hours. He was half awake, half asleep. He had to go to the bathroom but didn't want to move. He was waiting for the door to open. It was after ten and May, the receptionist, was probably late. He heard a moan from behind him and cocked his head in that direction. Helen was beginning to stir.

"Aspirin, I need aspirin, my brain's on fire," she was saying.

Scott stretched, heard his back crackle pop, then stood. "Is the office open today?"

"Weekday, isn't it?" Helen shot back. "Aspirin's in the bathroom."

He helped her to her feet. "Get it yourself."

She looked him straight in the eye. "I don't know who you are. I don't care either. Will you just get out of here?"

He started to help her to the bathroom. She backed away.

"Don't touch me. I'm sober now. Don't you touch me!"

"Look, Helen. We went through all this before. I don't want to hurt you. I'm looking for Jessica. I think she's in a lot of trouble and doesn't realize how bad the situation is. You could help by telling me where she is."

"You said you were a P.I., is that true?"

"I never said that." Scott paused. "I tell you what. I'll go if you recommend a place where I can get a room and some sleep, and if you promise to call me the minute Jessica returns. She is in trouble, Helen, serious trouble, and I believe I can help her before it's too late."

Her eyes widened. "Too late for what?"

"Who was she meeting in Miami?"

"A client."

"A client, in Miami?"

"Yeah, sure."

Scott put a hand on her shoulder. She stared him down. He pulled the hand away. "Remember, you're the one who told me you thought Jessica was in trouble. I work for the government, Helen. I'm here to help. Don't lie to me."

"The government." She laughed. "Which government?"

"Our government."

"Who's paying you the most?"

Scott squeezed his eyebrows together. "No one's paying me anything."

Helen started screaming, "I can't handle this. I need an aspirin. I need an aspirin."

"Get the whole bottle if it'll help."

"If May comes in, don't say anything about this to her."

He watched her slink away into the back room. He rubbed sleep from his eyes with the heels of his hands, then poured himself a cup of coffee. He kept an eye on the bathroom door in case there was a back exit he hadn't seen.

A few minutes later, she returned. She had rinsed the thick cake of makeup off her face, combed her hair, straightened her long, baggy dress. She looked younger, almost pretty.

She glanced at the wall clock. "May's not here yet?"

He nodded to the empty desk. "Is she usually late?"

"Never." Helen's jaw started to quiver. "I know he's paying

you, stop playing with me. Tell him I didn't tell you anything, and leave it at that. Tell him I'm willing to give him back the money. I don't want it. I'll never say anything, ever. I promise."

"Him?"

She glared. "Either way, you're here about WIH-2. Either way, I have nothing to say. Leave, please leave."

"You're worried about May and Jessica, aren't you?"

"Just get out of here." She broke into tears. "Tell him I wouldn't talk."

"I'm not leaving until I get what I came for."

There was sudden terror in her eyes. Her whole body started to tremble. She slapped her hands onto the desk. "I can't take it. Take my thumbs if you're going to. I don't want to conduct anymore. I can't hear the music, only the pain. Take them, tell him I didn't talk."

Scott wasn't sure if he should leave, embrace her, or just stand there. He put a hand on her shoulder. "I'm not here to hurt you, Helen. I'm not working for anyone that's going to hurt you. I won't let anyone hurt you."

She buried her face in his chest and continued sobbing. He embraced her awkwardly. She started kissing his cheek, pushed his hands to her breasts, then whispered in his ear, "Make me feel. I need to feel."

He put her at arm's length and gripped her elbows. "That's not what you need."

She started crying again.

"I saw a Hilton on the way into town. I'll check in. When you're ready to talk, call."

"Don't leave. I don't care who you're working for, don't leave me here alone." She sucked at the air nervously. "Where's May? If May was here everything would be all right."

Scott led Helen to the couch. He sat in an adjacent chair. "If you want me to stay, I need some answers. For starters, why did Jessica go to Miami and what did she bring back with her?"

"Jessica didn't come back from Miami."

Scott stood and started for the door. "When you're ready to tell the truth, call me."

"But that's the truth."

"And I suppose the wig and the attaché case in the other room are yours?"

"Wig?"

Scott opened the door. "The truth, when you're ready, call."

He walked out and closed the door behind him. He waited by the curb, pretending to fumble through his pockets for car keys. Eventually the door opened and Helen emerged. She held the wig in her hand.

"Jessica never wore this," she said, "but I don't suppose you'd understand why."

"Try me."

"Jessica's blonde."

Scott shot back, "Strawberry blonde since the day she was born, I know."

"Then what is this stuck to the hair tape?"

Scott spun around. "Black hair in the wig? That still doesn't mean…" Scott's voice trailed off. "You've never seen the case before?"

"Never."

Scott walked with Helen back into the reception area of J.

Wellmen & Associates. "Tell me everything, everything you know."

Helen's voice trembled as she said, "Jessica's alive, I know it."

Scott repeated, "Tell me everything."

Chapter 6

Miami, Florida
Monday, 3 January

Traffic on the Julia Tuttle Causeway was moderate, which wasn't surprising since it was almost 8 p.m. Still, Miami on a Monday night could hardly be called sleepy. East across Biscayne Bay lay Miami Beach and its five-star hotels, the type Jessica Wellmen preferred. "Life in the exclusive lane is where Jessica believes she belongs," Helen explained. Scott pretended to understand, but there was nothing in a five-star hotel that you couldn't find elsewhere for half the price.

Scott and Helen had danced in circles for hours, him digging for the truth, and her evading it. "Who is he and why are you so afraid of him?" he asked.

"A client," she answered.

"A client that threatened to cut off your thumbs?"

"Not the first time."

"All right, when was the first time you saw him?"

"Almost a year ago now."

"What is WIH-2?"

"Has to do with some gizmo Jessica made a test port for."

"A test port?"

"A box that checks a prototype gizmo."

"What about the money?"

"What money?"

"What about the missing days in the calendar?"

"May's job, not mine."

"Who erased the phone?"

"I don't know."

"Look, your sister's the one in trouble here. I'm just trying to help. Where are Jessica's files, her date book, her client list?"

"No matter whose side you're on, I've already said too much."

"Does Jessica have the box?"

"And if I said yes?"

"Will you help me find Jessica?"

"Only if you take me with you."

"Where?"

A short while later, they were on the road to Miami Beach in Scott's rented car. After that, Helen said only, "Wake me when we get there."

Scott glanced at her. Her seat was reclined all the way back. She seemed asleep, but he couldn't really be sure because she had a hand clutched over her face as if trying to ward off a pounding headache. He had a mounting headache of his own. Helen, teetering on the verge of a nervous breakdown, was the last thing he needed to worry about right now. There was no question in his mind that her emotional distress was real.

She was deathly afraid that anything she said would get Jessica killed. Yet, she was also hiding something—a secret so dark that she didn't want to share it with anyone, least of all herself. He couldn't help wondering if she had sold out her own sister and was now regretting the deed—money never satisfied over the long term. It just wasn't enough to help forget in the immediacy of the present.

He clicked on the radio, tuned up and down the dial to see what he could find. News Radio should have been somewhere in the low band on the AM dial. He glanced at Helen to see if the radio woke her. It didn't, but he wanted it to. He was on the other side of the bay now. The freeway was about to end, and he needed to know whether to turn north, south or continue to Collins Avenue. He nudged her. She jumped and shrank away.

He said, "Miami Beach."

In the rearview mirror as they passed under the street lights, he saw her face clearly. Her jaw was quivering, and she was trying to hide that fact, but her hand touched to her mouth was trembling right along with it.

"Helen, are you all right?"

"Don't touch me. Never touch me. I'm sober now. Keep your hands off me."

He said, his voice soft, "We're in Miami Beach."

She looked out the window. Her voice changed. "Good, the hotel. We're almost there."

"Directions," Scott shot back at her. "Are you going to help me out, or are we going to drive all night?"

Helen started crying.

Scott winced. He hadn't meant to snap at her. It just happened. "I'm sorry. Jessica did tell you which hotel she was going to check into?"

"She is my sister."

Scott looked at Helen sideways. "Is that a yes?"

"Yes, yes," and so saying, she finally gave him directions.

A short while later they were entering the lobby of the Miami Beach Ritz-Carlton. The lobby was immaculate and massive. Red carpets, crystal chandeliers everywhere. Five-star all the way. Scott turned up his nose and followed Helen to the front desk. Three night clerks were behind the desk. Helen approached one.

"A room?" the male clerk asked.

"Thank you, no."

His eyes lit up. "A suite, then?"

"Would you be a dear, I'm looking for my sister, Jessica Wellmen. She checked in on Thursday around midnight. Is she still registered at this hotel?"

"I can't give out a room number if that's what you're after. Against the rules, you know. We're very discreet."

"You *can* tell me if she checked in?"

"I suppose it wouldn't hurt." The clerk went over to a computer terminal. "Wellmen, Wellmen," he mumbled. "Sorry, no Wellmen."

"Maybe she checked out."

"I checked for Friday like you said."

"How about her mother's maiden name, Johnson?"

The clerk bobbed his head. "Jessica Johnson checked in on Thursday at 8:05 p.m. Paid for a week in advance."

"And the room number?"

"Already told you, against hotel policy. Discreet, we're very discreet. Take great pride in it. I can dial her room for you if you'd like? She can tell you herself then."

Scott leaned in close. "Can we talk privately?"

The clerk grinned and walked to the far end of the counter. He watched Scott's hands as if he expected something.

Scott leaned against the counter. "Can we keep this just between us?"

The clerk nodded greedily.

"I'm her husband, Bob. We're having difficulties. I'm afraid my wife is very distraught. She's diabetic, you know." He paused intentionally, then added, "She didn't take her insulin with her. I'm afraid—"

"Room 908," the clerk said in a hushed tone, "I'll make you a card key… I hope she's all right."

"I hope so too," Scott said, his voice grim.

The clerk made a card key. "Do you want me to call the paramedics, just in case?"

"No, no. Helen here knows how to administer the insulin. Things'll be fine now. Thank you. You may have saved my wife's life."

The desk clerk stood a little taller. "If there's anything you need, anything at all, call down to the front desk, and I'll see you get it."

Scott and Helen went to the elevator. The elevator doors opened on the ninth floor. Neither had spoken during the brief ride, and the closer they got to Room 908, the faster Helen's jaw quivered.

He said, "If there's something you haven't told me, now would be a good time."

She looked up at him. Her eyes full of tears. "She really is diabetic, you know. I don't want to know if it was a guess or if you actually knew, but I hope nothing else you said comes true. Jessica's all I have left, except maybe May, but May's not family."

"I'll take that as a no," Scott mumbled. He passed the card key through the reader, looked up and down the hall to make sure it was empty, then took out his gun. He looked directly at Helen. "Stay here until I say otherwise."

He turned the knob and slowly opened the door. The room was dark. The NVGs were still in the car, he hadn't expected to find a darkened room. He didn't know if it was a good sign or a bad sign, but he didn't wait to find out. He slipped into the room and eased the door closed behind him. His heart was racing in his ears. He felt strange, good. The way he always felt during a mission—but usually not after.

He crouched to his knees and made his way through the room an inch at a time. His eyes adjusted to the darkness, but everything was still bathed in shadows. A bathroom door was to his right, he continued past it.

He sniffed the air. He didn't smell anything. No perfume, no aftershave, not even the scent of shampoo from the bathroom. He continued into the room. Closets came next on the left, a bed was on the right. He snaked around the right side of the bed, raised his hands to where a person's head should have been and found nothing. He circled to the left side of the bed, and again found nothing. The bed was empty, that didn't mean the room was.

A lamp was next to the bed. He put his back to the wall and switched it on. Gun at the ready, he turned it in a swift 180 around the room. The room was thankfully empty. He looked under the bed. He went to the bathroom and jolted the door open. The bathroom was empty. The shower walls were dry. He checked the closets next and found empty hangers.

He opened the door and waved Helen in. "No one's here. The bed hasn't been slept in recently. The shower walls are dry. No clothes in the closet."

She buried her face in his chest. She whispered, "Make me feel. I need to feel."

He put her at arm's length. "You're tired. You don't know what you want. Rest, I'll see if I can find out the last time Jessica was seen here in the hotel. Do you have a picture of her in your purse?"

Helen began unbuttoning her dress. Scott touched his hand to hers as a sign to stop. She smiled, slipped the dress off her shoulders and it fell to the floor. She wasn't wearing a bra, only panties with a lace band. Her figure was nothing like the baggy clothes had suggested and everything like the name Helen suggested. She was striking, beautiful, vulnerable.

She took his hand and pulled him against her. She kissed him on the lips. He kissed her forehead.

She lay down, pulling him with her. She started unbuttoning his shirt, unzipped his pants and all the while, blew gently in his ear.

He was aroused, couldn't help but be aroused, and it made what he had to do all the more difficult. His body tensed all over.

He started to stand.

"Don't leave me," she whispered. "Please, I don't want to be alone. Just close your eyes and go with it."

"Go with it?"

"That's what he told me when he raped me. Take the pain away. I want to feel. I want to hear the music."

He closed his eyes and inhaled deeply. She continued blowing in his ear. But it wasn't going to happen, not now, not ever. He rolled over onto the other side of the bed but kept his arm around her. "I'm not going to leave you, Helen. You sleep now."

For a long time she trembled. He kept his arm around her and stared up at the ceiling. He tried to imagine the warm body beside him was Cynthia's, but that didn't help anything. He wished he didn't need Helen to find Jessica, but for the time being it was good that they needed each other. If Jessica was dead, Helen was his only link to the killer, the assignment, the whole mess.

Eventually he slept, but only for a few hours. He awoke around eleven and knew the entire night was ahead.

He found Helen's purse and rummaged through it. Hidden in a side pocket was a small .22 gun. He wasn't surprised. He found a few pictures: One of her and Jessica—there was a strong family resemblance. She had twenty-seven dollars in her billfold, a few dollars in coins in the change compartment. He didn't find any drugs, not even prescription, which did surprise him. And there was a note:

Helen, see you Sunday at Pete's.
Celebration. Bring your happy mood.

He glanced over to the bed. Helen was still asleep. She had kicked the blankets off, and her breasts were like beacons. He decided to take a cold shower.

He was stepping out of the shower, reaching for a towel, when he saw it. It was barely visible under the clear plastic garbage bag, but it was there. He dried himself quickly, wrapped the towel around his waist. He lifted the bag out of the trash can, revealing a covered dish. The kind room service used. He smiled, hurried out of the bathroom. His suit was draped over a chair. He was putting on his boxers when he heard her shift in the bed.

"Nice," she said, "very nice. Bring those muscles back over here."

He continued dressing. "Give it a rest, Helen. Go back to sleep."

She started crying.

"Are you seeing a therapist?"

"No head shrinker can tell me what's wrong with me. I know, I know all too well."

"You'd be surprised. You're confused. You need help."

She pulled the bed sheet over her head. "Where are you going?"

"I think I have a lead. Sleep, we'll talk in the morning."

He finished dressing, then waited to make sure she went back to sleep. He grabbed the covered dish from the trash can and made his way to the lobby. Only two clerks were behind the desk now. One of them was the clerk he spoke to earlier.

He slammed the plate onto the counter. "Who made this delivery?"

The clerk came over. "Is there something wrong, sir?"

"Yes, there is." He scowled. "I need to know when this was delivered. Her blood-sugar level is all messed up, and you did it!"

"I would ask you to lower your voice, sir."

"Lower my voice? How's this?" Scott shouted.

The clerk went over to the computer terminal. "Jessica Johnson, right?"

"Yes!"

"There was a request for room service around eleven forty-five on Friday night, but I don't think that—"

"Do you presume to tell me about my own wife now?" Scott glared. "Who made the delivery?"

"Probably a bellboy. You're not going to do anything violent, are you?"

Scott shook his head, apparently he was playing the part a little too well. "I just need to know if he saw her eat it."

"Check the kitchen, right through there." The clerk pointed.

Scott nodded and trotted off. The kitchen was nearly deserted. The solitary cook looked at him quizzically.

Scott said, "Who makes night deliveries for room service?"

"If you wanted room service, you could have called down."

"No, I need to know the name of a bellboy that made a delivery to Room 908 on Friday night around twelve."

"This is a joke, right?"

"There's a Benjamin Franklin in it, if I get a name."

"The money first."

Scott took a crisp hundred-dollar bill out of his wallet.

"If she signed a tip to the bill, the bellhop would've signed to claim it."

Scott snatched the money away from the cook's reaching hand. "No name, no game."

"What shit is this? That's the best I can do."

Scott waved the hundred-dollar bill like a tiny flag. "You could get a name for me, if you wanted to, couldn't you?"

The cook picked up a nearby phone, dialed. "Yeah, I got a customer complaint. Claims someone signed a big tip to the room service bill. I need the bellhop's name… Friday night, Room 908…" The cook hung up the phone, turned back to Scott, screamed, "Ernie, delivery!"

Scott handed the cook the money.

A pimple-faced teenager came running into the kitchen. Scott met the kid halfway, flashed a Ben Franklin at him and walked into the hall. The kid followed.

"You a cop," Ernie said, "I hate cops. I won't talk if you're a cop."

Scott waved the bill in front of Ernie's dazzled eyes. "No cop. Do you remember a delivery you made to Room 908 on Friday?"

"I make a lot of deliveries."

Scott showed him the picture of Helen and Jessica. Ernie's face flushed red. "You remember something?"

"I saw her all right." He reached for the money.

"There's more, I know there's more."

Ernie whispered, "There's two of them in there, right? They're getting it on. I can hear it through the door. I knock anyway. They ordered food, right?"

"And?"

"She tells me to set it outside the door and I do, then I left. You going to give me the hundred or not?"

"And?"

"I was walking down the hall, right? I hear the door open, so I look back. She opens the door and reaches out to get the food."

"And?"

"What are you, a priest? You want a confession?"

"If you've got something to confess."

"She looks at me and smiles this big smile… She isn't wearing anything at the time. That's why I remember. All right?"

Scott pointed to the picture. "And this is the woman you saw?"

"I wasn't exactly looking at her face, but yeah, that's her."

Scott gave Ernie the money and turned away.

Ernie said, "Who is she anyway?"

"My wife," Scott shot back, "my wife."

Ernie gulped and dashed into the kitchen.

Scott slowly made his way back to Room 908. He didn't take the elevator this time. He took the stairs. The exercise was therapeutic and he needed to think.

Helen was sound asleep when he entered the room. He knew there was nothing he could do until morning, so he lay down on the bed. With his arms crossed behind his head, he stared into the darkness and at the ceiling he could see only vaguely. Sometime after 2 a.m., he fell asleep, must have. But when he awoke, it didn't seem like he had slept at all. And yet there was sunshine poking through the curtains, so he must have.

The bed seemed cold. He reached out and found Helen was gone. He jumped out of bed, ran for the door, and was about to open it when he noticed the bathroom light was on. He listened at the door. There was no water running, and it didn't sound like anyone was on the toilet.

He called out, "Helen, are you in there?"

"Yep… I'm here."

He said through the closed door, "Who's Pete? Jessica's boyfriend?"

Helen laughed. "The bar where I got drunk on Sunday night. Why?"

"The note in your purse. Was it from Jessica?"

"You went through my purse?"

"I was looking for the pictures of Jessica. Look, does she have a boyfriend?"

"Jessica, a boyfriend?" Helen laughed again. "She doesn't date men."

"Would she have met someone here on Friday night?"

Silence greeted him.

"Helen?"

He opened the door slowly. She was curled up in a corner next to the tub, crying and trembling. He coaxed her out of the corner and into a chair. He opened the curtains so the warm sunshine bathed her face. Later he ordered room service for two—steak, eggs, pancakes, hash browns, a pitcher of orange juice—and of course charged it to the room.

When the food came, Helen picked at it. Scott ended up eating more than he should have, and there were still lots of leftovers. The only thing he finished was the pitcher of O.J., which he couldn't seem to get enough of.

He waited until Helen looked relaxed, then asked about Jessica's girlfriends. Jessica had only one, and no, Pattie didn't live in Miami. She didn't live in Florida, either. She flew in sometimes on weekends and that was about all Helen knew about Pattie.

Scott excused himself to make a phone call. He told her not to go anywhere. She promised she wouldn't.

The pay phone in the lobby wasn't his first stop. He bought a newspaper first, scanned the headlines, the obits. No murders, no suicides, no Jane Doe's. He wasn't surprised to find that *it* had happened again. In his mind's eye, he saw the billions the several-minute-long outage had wiped out. He saw the controlling hands tighten their grip and he was more terrified than when he'd been crawling on his belly with car bombs exploding all around him.

Surviving Munich had been skill and luck, but things were different now. Now the lines were blurred and he wasn't sure who was playing who. The only thing he knew for sure was that Glen had brought him back in for a reason and that Glen had given him this assignment for a reason. If he wanted to stay alive—if he wanted those he cared about to stay alive—he'd play the game but knew he was playing for all the wrong reasons.

He was about to use the phone when he saw a man heading toward the elevators. He recognized the face from somewhere. He took a second look. The man had the skin tone and hair color of a Pacific Islander, was built like a Samoan, but didn't carry himself like a Samoan. He walked with purpose, not like a man on island time.

Scott decided to follow. The guy saw him, continued past the elevators and stopped in front of the door to the stairs. Scott came up alongside him. "You deliver pizzas to Miami Beach too?"

The guy looked at Scott like he was strange. "You thinking of someone else."

The guy started to walk off. Scott grabbed him by the shirt, picked him up off the floor and tossed him at the door to the stairs. The door opened. Scott's momentum carried him through it to the wall of the stairwell. "Who are you and why are you following me?"

"Keneke Kawena."

"Just what is that?"

"My name, Keneke Kawena."

Scott's nostrils flared.

"I work for HPD."

"HPD?"

"Honolulu Police Department." Keneke took out his badge and showed it to Scott.

Scott felt relief. He let go of the guy's shirt and took a step back. "Why are you following me, detective? Aren't you a little out of your jurisdiction?"

"You call me Ken, and I'm not a detective, yet. I'm a computer technician assigned to the fraud division."

"Fraud? Look, Ken, I'm in a hurry. Are you following me?"

"The cuckoo's egg."

"Come again?"

"The cuckoo's egg."

"Look, I'm on vacation. If you're some kind of nut case, that's fine by me, but go bother someone else."

"I'm gone. You'll never see me again."

Scott said dryly, "That would be wonderful."

Ken walked off. Scott sulked for a moment. Wondered if he was getting paranoid. Wondered if Glen had sent Ken to check up on him, then went into the hall.

Two pay phones were off the lobby. Someone was using one. He could have used the other, but didn't want to talk while anyone was within earshot. He remembered seeing a phone booth on the street near the hotel. He went outside and walked about half a block. Thankfully no one was using the phone.

He called Glen at the office. Glen's secretary told him, "Mr. Hastings is still at home." He dialed Glen's home number, but the line was busy. As he waited to try again, it started to rain.

The second time he tried, he got through. He yelled into the receiver, "Did you send some idiot down here to check up on me?"

Glen didn't say anything.

"Well, did you?"

"Scott," Glen said, clear tension in his voice, "I think you should come back to Baltimore."

"Why?"

"I think I should tell you this in person."

"Tell me now, Glen. I'm close to something. I can feel it. A few more days, that's all."

"Scott, where are you? Are you sitting?"

"Don't play melodrama with me. It's not you. Spit it out, I'm listening."

There was silence on the other end of the line for a moment. Glen said, "There's been an accident. Cynthia's in the hospital. I think you should fly back to Baltimore on the next flight."

For an instant, Scott saw his father's face. Heard the snap of the trigger and the explosion of the gun firing.

"Scott, are you there?"

"Which hospital?"

Glen told him.

Scott hung up and raced to the hotel. Helen seemed to recognize the alarm on his face right away. He didn't have to tell her he was leaving. She knew. She wanted to go with him. She didn't want to be alone. She told him that she had proof that Jessica had the gizmo with her and that it was worth a lot more than anyone knew.

He asked her if she had a safe place to stay, a place that wasn't in Miami or Boca Raton. She said she knew a place no one would think to look for her. He gave her enough cab fare to take her to the Georgia state line, even though she was only going to Tampa. She wrote down the phone number. He put her in a cab and told her to stay out of sight until he came for her.

Chapter 7

Baltimore, Maryland
Tuesday, 4 January

Glen sank into the folds of the black leather chair, then purposefully plopped his feet onto the top of the massive mahogany desk that dominated his office. He didn't care that his shoes were caked with mud or that one of the little people would have to clean up the mess. He glanced at the umbrella and the puddle forming beneath it. Damned rain just wouldn't end.

The phone rang. Glen snatched it up, then waited for the Christmas tree of indicators on a box attached to the phone to light all the way to the top. Once he was sure he was on a clear, untapped line, he grinned into the video phone and said, "Did you do it?"

"Is it safe?"

Glen beaded his eyes.

"All right, stupid question—"

"You're right, it was. Did you do it?"

"The money. You said we'd talk money now."

"You give me what I want, and by close of business, there'll be a hundred thousand in your account. Does that make you happy?"

"I think two is a better number."

Glen slammed the phone on the desk a few times. The video screen cracked and blanked out. He whispered into the phone, "Now you listen to me and listen close. That's the only offer. Try a double cross and they'll find you wrapped in your intestines. Do we understand each other?"

"You're right, absolutely right. One is a fair number. I did it, I have everything you requested."

"And the dosages?"

"All written down, just like you requested."

"Is it traceable?"

"We're talking pharmaceuticals, not bullets. Traceable to the manufacturer, hell yes. Traceable to you, never."

"You haven't told anyone else about this?"

"I'm not stupid. I know better than to shoot off my mouth. I—"

"Make the delivery when and where we discussed. The money will be transferred to your account. You have my word."

Glen smiled as he hung up the phone. He took the pistol out of the top desk drawer and sighted it on the door. The gun wasn't loaded, but he wished it were. He squeezed the trigger. The pull seemed a little heavy. He squeezed the trigger again. Yes, definitely heavy.

He dismantled the gun, set about adjusting the trigger pull. He liked to think of the act of squeezing the trigger as effortless and that he need only breathe on the gun to make it fire. There was no point making something work that wasn't.

Satisfied, he put the gun away and started dialing the phone. "On the way," he said once the Christmas tree lights were full on.

"What does he know?"

Glen leaned back in the chair. "I don't think he knows anything."

"You're sure?"

"After all we've been through, you have to ask?"

"It's what I do. I'll see you this afternoon then?"

"Wouldn't miss it."

Glen hung up the phone and dialed another number. He didn't wait for the lights; the line wasn't verifiable. "Are you ready?"

"Ready as I'll ever be. Why do bad things have to happen to good people?"

"I'll pick you up in an hour, at four. He'll be there before us. I need you to be strong when you see him. Can you do that for me, Janet?"

"I'm your girl, aren't I?"

"That's my girl. You going to wear the yellow dress?"

"Glen."

"For me."

"I will if you want me to, but it's hardly appropriate."

"It's a long drive."

"Okay, you win. Can I ever resist?"

"See you at four." Glen hung up the phone and turned to the window.

***

Scott sucked at the air in short, rapid puffs, his hand on the door handle. He promised himself he wanted to go in, promised himself he was ready to go in, but felt like he was suffocating. His chest was tight. His head was about to explode. Old and painful memories haunted his thoughts. The cab ride from the airport to the hospital in bumper-to-bumper traffic hadn't helped anything.

The cab's meter, a testament to how long he had been trapped in the back seat, read one hundred ninety-six dollars. In the last half hour, it seemed the cab moved only inches, and all he could think about the entire time was Cynthia and the baby.

He was angry, and mashing his fist into the armrest didn't help. He didn't understand why anyone'd go after Cynthia and the baby. He was playing the game. He'd come back in. He'd done the right thing. There could be no doubt about loyalty.

He called the hospital more than a dozen times from the Miami airport, from the Sky Phone, and upon arrival in Baltimore. Cynthia's attending physician was Dr. Maureen Fitzpatrick. He still hadn't been able to speak with her personally, but he knew both the family physician, Dr. Emery Haskins, and Cynthia's gynecologist, Dr. William Brown, had been consulted.

Cynthia had been moved from intensive care to a private monitored room. Her condition, serious and marginally stable as of a few hours ago, was critical before he departed Miami. But he knew from experience that the difference between marginally stable and worse was a few heartbeats and that the difference between life and death was but a single heartbeat.

He closed his eyes and tried to picture Cynthia as he had seen her last. He could recall every detail vividly. Her long brown hair cast over her left shoulder. Her brown eyes, sad. Her lipstick, a shade less than rose. Her perfume, flowery, sweet and exotic. But the face before his eyes was his father's and not Cynthia's. The doctors had been full of hope then, too. "The bullet went through clean, Scott. There's no hemorrhaging. It's a miracle." If it was a miracle, then why was he at a funeral forty-eight hours later?

He exhaled, was about to open the door, when he heard a woman's voice calling his name. At first he thought he imagined the voice, but then he heard it again.

"Mr. Evers, Dr. Maureen Fitzpatrick. I came as soon as Mr. Simons told me you had arrived. Can we talk a moment before you go in? Has anyone told you about your wife's condition?"

He released his grip on the door handle, felt the blood rush back into his hand. "Dr. Fitzpatrick?"

He turned. There was an awkward moment as Scott wondered if he should shake her extended hand or not, then he shook her hand.

Dr. Fitzpatrick said, "You look exhausted. Come with me. We'll sit and talk for a moment."

"Why is it that everyone knows about my wife's condition but me?"

"I think it best if we go sit."

"Why did they move her to a private room if her condition is still serious?"

"Mr. Simons requested it."

"Is Mr. Simons her husband?"

She glanced at her watch. "I believe we're getting off to a bad start. Your wife was in a terrible accident. Her air bag didn't open. She's lucky to be alive. I think we should go down to the lounge."

Despite his training, his knees started to buckle under his weight. "I think that would be good."

Dr. Fitzpatrick led Scott to a private lounge. She started to pull out charts, he stopped her.

He said, "Just give it to me straight."

She suggested he sit. He didn't but he did prepare to hear something he didn't want to hear. For a moment it was as if he were reliving high school. His freshman year had been full of ups and downs. His father had retired from the military that June, blew his brains out with a shotgun that August.

Everything changed after that. The extrovert, the jock and the guy everyone liked went away. An introvert, a rebel, a guy no one wanted to know took his place. Truancy records and police reports replaced honor roll lists and martial arts trophies. A one-way ticket to Pendleton Military School followed. But Pendleton wasn't his saving grace. It only taught him that weapons and tactics could resolve things he couldn't hope to resolve otherwise.

As Dr. Fitzpatrick spoke, he heard but didn't truly hear. "We tried to save them both, but couldn't. The trauma of the impact was too much." She put a hand on his shoulder. "We lost the baby."

He tried to sit but found his legs were rooted to the floor. "And Cynthia?"

"She doesn't know. She hasn't regained consciousness yet."

"Will she live?"

"She's a fighter. Once we made the decision to perform surgery, things shifted in her favor."

He asked to be alone and Dr. Fitzpatrick left saying how sorry she was, but how lucky he was. Cynthia should recover and in time they could try to have another child. He didn't say anything but wished for her optimism. Afterward he stood motionless for a long time. He didn't sit, couldn't sit. He just stood there, staring blankly at the wall.

And then for a second time he found himself standing outside Cynthia's hospital room, afraid to go in, afraid not to. He took a deep breath, opened the door. A dim lamp was turned on beside her bed.

For a fleeting moment, he saw the wires, the machines, the IV feeding her intravenously and afterward, all he could see was the image of her face in his mind's eye the last time he saw her. Her beautiful brown eyes, sad. The lipstick on her lips a shade less than rose. Her long brown hair draped over her left shoulder. He even imagined he could smell her perfume, exotic, sweet, flowery.

He crossed to the bed, kissed her cheek. Her skin was clammy. Her eyes, bruised and swollen. Her lips, dry and cracked. Her head, wrapped in bandages. He kissed her cheek again, closed his eyes, and did a thing he'd never done before. He prayed, a real prayer, not a momentary fleeting prayer, but a real prayer.

Through the night, he stayed at her bedside. Daddy Simons came and went. The doctors came and went. Glen and Janet stopped in for a few minutes. Janet told him it was a good thing Glen had been there to call the paramedics. But he didn't see any of them. He only saw her lying supine on the hospital bed. The color gone from her face. The bruises deepening under her eyes. Every hour that passed made him more angry, more sure that her accident wasn't an accident.

***

Outside the broad windows of the den, the rain had finally stopped. Janet put three ice cubes in a glass, poured the scotch and added a splash of water. Glen watched. He liked to watch her move amidst the red-orange glow cast by the fire. The light danced off her thighs and back, revealing the subtleties of her curves.

She grinned as she swished across the room and slid in beside him on the floor. She handed him the glass and nibbled his ear while he sipped his drink and the logs in the hearth slowly melted to fiery ashes.

Later, Glen watched Janet stew over a question he knew she wanted to ask. And then when he thought she wouldn't say anything, she whispered, "Do you think he got the message?"

"One thing for certain, when it clicks, he'll come running."

"Do you want me to leave?"

"You do have an early day tomorrow."

"This is hard on you, isn't it?" She massaged his neck muscles.

"Not like the old days. They were on one side. We were on the other."

"Times changed. The whole world changed."

"The dinosaurs are still the same. The game changed. We didn't."

She stood, started dressing. "I'll call you Friday when I get back."

"Call me before then."

"Don't worry. You taught me everything I know, remember?"

Glen grinned. "How could I forget?"

She slipped on her black leather pumps. He walked her to the door. They were in the middle of a kiss when someone pounded on the door. Glen told her, "Go out the back door," then clicked on the front porch light when she reached it. He shouted, "Just a minute," as he started to dress.

Glen chuckled when he heard Scott shouting, "Open the door or I'll bust it in!"

He turned on the den lights and put his drink away while he waited to see if Scott *could* break down the door. There were two deadbolts on it, so he seriously doubted if anyone could break it down, but if Scott wanted to try, why not let him.

A moment later he heard a crack, and the wooden door frame came splintering inward. He nodded approval as he ambled to the foyer, grinning toothily and waiting for Scott's fist to wipe the grin away.

The blow knocked Glen to the floor. Scott continued screaming and towered over him. "You son of a bitch! You did it, didn't you? You threatened to do it and you did it. I ought to kill you, right now, right here, just to see how many people would thank me!"

Glen shook his head and struggled from the floor.

Scott knocked him down again. "Don't move. I'm not done yet."

Glen moaned. "I think you broke my jaw." He tried to stand. Scott tried to hit him. He blocked. Two blows to the face were enough for any martyr. They struggled. Scott's hands were around Glen's throat.

"If she dies, I'll make you feel everything she felt!"

Glen broke free, rolled, came up on his feet. He proclaimed his innocence while he held Scott's fist at bay. "I made a mistake before. You've got to believe me when I say I'd never cross the line. I'd never hurt Cynthia. I was the one who introduced you to her, for chrissakes. I made an empty and stupid threat that I've regretted ever since. I did it because I needed you on the team. Do you think I'm an idiot? I need you in Miami, not here in Baltimore sitting beside a hospital bed. You know what's going on."

Scott looked confused for a moment, but that didn't stop him from landing a kick to the head that knocked Glen off his feet. He towered over Glen, looking down. "I suppose you just happened to be there when it happened?"

"I need you in Miami, not here in Baltimore sitting beside a hospital bed," Glen repeated as he shook his head and held his jaw. "I really think you broke it. Quite a kick."

"Why were you there?"

"Let's sit. Can we sit?" Glen staggered to the couch. Scott sat across from him. "Cynthia was worried about you, that's why."

Scott's expression revealed his disbelief.

Glen continued, "I get this message on my answering machine to call the Chairman at once. So I called, and that's how it all started. Cynthia was worried about you. I met her and we talked. I left. She left. We both happened to be going the same direction: Back to 695. That tanker truck driver never slowed down. The police report says it all. If I hadn't been able to pull her out just before the explosion, I wouldn't be here either. We'd both be dead."

Scott buried his head in his hands. "If anything happens to her, I don't know what I'll do. I can't think. I can't sleep. I can't eat."

Glen reached out to Scott. "That's exactly what they wanted."

Scott shot back, "What do you mean?"

"You said yourself you were close to something." The phone rang. Glen ignored it, continued. "They wanted you off the trail and brought you all the way back to Baltimore. They're good, indisputably good. We can't let this go on. This is our only lead. The connection to Munich has to be obvious to you now."

"Munich?"

"Yes, Munich. What did you think? Why do you think I need you? You're the one, Scott. You got closer in this than anyone— and you came back. You're the one who can put the pieces together. I'm counting on it and so are a lot of other people."

Scott jumped up. He'd known there was a connection, but if this was connected to Munich, Munich was connected to Paris and Paris to Berlin. "How far back does this go?"

Glen knew that the pieces were coming together for Scott. "Been chasing this ghost my whole career, so have you and a dozen like you. I knew in '87 we were close to something but Black Monday happened anyway."

"Why me?"

Glen walked to the table and unrolled a map of the world. "Teams and operations. Positive identifications and links. A lifetime's work, the whole of their network. The magic question remains—"

"Who's at the top? Who's pulling the strings?"

"Exactly."

Scott rubbed his eyes. "Glen, I don't know what to say. I'm not thinking straight. I just made an ass of myself. Do you want some ice?" The phone started ringing again. "Do you want me to answer that?"

"Could you pour me a scotch? Nice and stiff. I'll get the phone."

Glen waited until Scott was on the other side of the room, then answered the phone. He didn't say anything immediately. His desk phone took a little longer than the video phone in his office to verify the line. "Hello?"

The voice on the other end of the line said, "I did it."

"You closed the deal?"

Silence greeted him.

"Did you close the deal or not?"

"Yes. He enjoyed it. I enjoyed it. We did it all night if that's what you want to hear. Does that make you happy, you sick—"

Glen clamped a hand over the receiver. He said to Scott, "I'm sorry, I have to take this. Pour yourself a drink. You look like you need it." Into the receiver he said, "And the records?"

"Let me talk to her."

Out of the corner of his eye, Glen saw Scott pour straight bourbon into a glass and gulp it down. "Deliver them, then you'll get what you want."

"I want to hear her voice. I have to know—"

Glen waved and smiled as Scott poured another drink for himself then started putting ice into another glass. "One word, one more word, and I'll send something back to you that you'll swear is a jigsaw puzzle and not a human being."

He heard sobbing on the other end of the line.

"Deliver the records!" Glen slammed the phone down. He walked back to the couch. Scott was staring blankly at the wall. He picked up the drink Scott made for him and held it against his jaw.

Scott looked him straight in the eye. "Let's level the playing field. You tell me everything you haven't told me about John Ellis Wellmen. Everything."

"There's a lot more than you can handle, and sometimes when you know too much, you wish you didn't know anything at all."

"I'm not going anywhere until you tell me everything."

Glen walked to his desk, unlocked a drawer, and removed it from the desk. A large manila envelope was taped to the bottom of the drawer. "Ever heard of the People's Armed Police?"

"Extremists. Isn't there supposed to be a link between them and the importing of weapons into the U.S.?"

Glen smiled. Scott wasn't an expert on arms, but he understood the playing field. "No supposedly about it. It's a multibillion-dollar industry, and it's all very legal." He handed Scott the envelope. "These documents date back to the early '80's."

Scott was hesitant to open it. Glen indicated it was all right. Scott thumbed through the thick stack of documents. "What's this? Everything anyone'd ever want to know about the arms business but were afraid to ask?"

"Not everything, and only the dealings we're tracking."

Scott gulped down Glen's drink. Glen didn't comment. Scott

said, "Just how does all this relate? This isn't about weapons. This is about something else entirely."

"Are you so sure?" Glen eyed the photograph in Scott's hands. He tapped the map, didn't say anything more immediately, then stood. "You want another drink?"

"Just bring the bottle."

Glen knew Scott meant the bottle of bourbon. He made himself a drink and brought the bourbon for Scott. He sucked at his drink, dug his fist into the couch. "Billions weren't enough for our Mr. Wellmen. He wanted to control an empire in the heart of the United States of America, and we let him."

"Meaning?"

"He saw a way to make billions, simply and all very legal. Our government has known for a very long time of companies with ties to extremists. The extremists conduct business through these companies. They use the companies to recruit, to set up more businesses, the more legitimate the better, and then use these businesses as cover."

"Skip to the part where you tell me about Wellmen. You think he's the one?"

"I am telling you about Wellmen. Profits and greed are the order of the day, as it's always been. Nothing's changed."

Scott held up the picture. "And this?"

"Pretty, isn't it? I always liked a picture of an explosion and there was none better than a perfect mushroom cloud…"

"How does this relate to Wellmen?"

"Seismographs all over the world picked it up moments after it occurred."

"The box in Florida's a bomb?"

Glen knew every word in the document attached to the photo. He'd read it hundreds of times late at night. He said quietly, "We knew the day, the hour, the instant it happened, but we couldn't do anything about it."

Scott shouted, "This is about a nuclear bomb?"

Glen laughed. "Compared to Wellmen, bomb-toting wackos are amateur hour. Why use a bomb when you've got a better weapon? A weapon that leaves no trail, doesn't harm the innocent but can topple governments."

"Damned booze," Scott cursed as he threw the bottle of bourbon across the room. It shattered the glass mirror behind the bar. "Do I have your attention now?"

Glen was wide-eyed and more than a little irritated. First the front door and now this. "You've had my attention. Don't forget who's in control here. I give the orders. You follow them."

Scott picked up Glen's glass and dumped the contents on the floor. "If you say so."

Glen knew he was being played right then. "You want to know about the box. I'll tell you. Don't blame me if it comes back to bite you in the ass."

"The box."

"High-tech, next generation, A.I. fuzzy logic heart. It's the next piece they need." Glen hurled his empty glass at the bricks above the fireplace.

Scott smiled. "Maid's gonna love you."

"Get this bastard, Scott. Find the box. Follow the trail. Trace it all back to Wellmen. Let us take care of the rest."

Scott leaned forward, pursed his lips. "Is Wellmen the one?"

"Have you been listening to anything I've said?"

Scott nodded. "Spell it out for me. I want to hear you say it."

"Scott, get back down to Florida. Get these sons of bitches. Get them for me. Get them for Cynthia. Get them for yourself. Get them."

Chapter 8

Tampa, Florida
Friday, 7 January

Scott dropped the bottle, heard it shatter when it hit the concrete. The flight to Tampa International had been awful and turbulent. He spent most of the time in the bathroom. He staggered up to the second floor of a small rundown apartment building, lost his liquid lunch over the railing, then pounded on the door to Apartment 2E.

No one answered.

He continued pounding.

Scott stopped when he thought he heard a voice. The door opened a crack.

He saw the chain was on, didn't care, and kicked the door open. He backed Helen into the couch with his eyes, put his hands around her throat and squeezed.

"Now we're going to have a conversation," he said. "I ask the questions. You provide the answers. Do you understand?"

Helen bobbed her head. Scott liked the terror in her eyes and the fact that he liked it surprised him.

"Have you seen Jessica?"

Helen sucked at her lip and shook her head.

"Where is Jessica?"

"I don't know."

"How can I reach Pattie?"

"I don't know."

He smacked her backhanded across the face. "Where is Jessica's date book? Where are the files?"

Her eyes darted around the room. "I don't know."

He smacked her again. For an instant, it seemed the room moved.

She tried to kiss his mouth. He pushed her away.

"How much did they pay you to lie to me?"

"No one paid me to lie."

He let her go. Her eyes widened. He staggered toward the door. "I don't need you. You need me. Remember that when they find Jessica floating face down."

She ran after him. She grabbed his hand and pulled him against her.

The room shifted under his feet. Scott wobbled and started to fall. Helen supported him. The room had a ceiling fan, he saw suddenly. It was going round and round and round.

"Scott, stay with me," she said. She draped his arm around her shoulder and helped him into the other room.

Everything was moving. A door opened. There was a bed. He fell onto it face first. Everything went black.

Hours later, he smelled something, opened his eyes, tried to sit up, found it difficult. Helen was standing over him in her underwear. He rubbed his eyes with the heels of his hands. He was lying in bed with a sheet over him. His clothes were in a heap on the floor. She stuck a plate of food into his hand.

He took the plate, set it next to him, then looked under the sheet to see whether he was really naked or not. "We didn't?"

She handed him a cup. "We did."

He took a sip and spit. "Bourbon."

"Water."

"Bourbon, get me a bottle. I'm not going to do anything today sober."

"You're an angry, mean S.O.B. when you're drunk. You'll get no booze from me." She threw a bottle of pills at him.

He looked at it. "Midol?"

"Maybe it'll cure more than your hangover."

He tugged at his hair. "We didn't really, did we?"

"Eat. It's getting cold. You should be hungry."

He collapsed back on the bed, set the cup on his forehead. The cool oozed out of the cup and into his aching head.

He was famished, hated the fact that he was, hated the thoughts running through his aching brain. There was no denying the fact that Helen aroused his sense of curiosity. But if he had slept with her, he should remember something. He remembered nothing, nothing since Baltimore. Frustrated, he screamed, "Put some clothes on!"

He winced, tried to hold his brains in as his head started throbbing, but nothing worked.

"Take the Midol," Helen recommended.

He tried to open the bottle, but his hands just wouldn't work. Helen opened the bottle and gave him two pills. He wanted three or four, but she said two would work just fine. Afterward, she fed him while he lay on his back.

He asked her later, "What happened yesterday? I don't even remember this room."

Helen said, quiet and firm, "If you ever hurt me again, I'll find a way to kill you. I will."

She had a fork in one hand, a knife in the other. He edged away from her. "That wasn't me yesterday, Helen."

"I think it was, especially when we got around to it."

His eyes showed disbelief.

She used his confusion and kissed him on the mouth. She crawled up on top of him, peeled off her bra, placed his hands on her breasts. "You like the feel of them, don't you? Want to try to get it right this time? I can tell you're a real ladies' man."

He put his hands to his head. The room was spinning. She kissed her way down to his belly. He tried to push her away. She held on and went at it with even more vigor. He grabbed the mattress with both hands as she moved faster and faster. For a few moments, the pounding in his head went away.

When it was over, she giggled and worked her way back to his mouth. She said, "Now it's the truth and not a lie, and no one will hurt Jessica."

"What the hell is that supposed to, to—" he stopped tried to think of what he was going to say, "to mean?"

"I did, you didn't. You did, I didn't." She wiped her lips, put her bra back on and left the room.

He wanted to chase after her, but found his shoulders were too heavy to lift off the bed and his eyes, he just couldn't keep them open. He used one hand to hold the other while he forced his droopy eyelids open. "Did you put something in that?"

"Night night," Helen shouted back at him. "Sleep tight. You were marvelous, baby, marvelous."

Chapter 9

Tampa, Florida
Sunday, 9 January

"A truce," Scott told her as he sat up. Helen sat down on the bed. He took in the deep purple bruises on her neck and the thick makeup on her cheeks and eyes. "My head is killing me, and no, I don't want anything for it."

She whispered, "You hurt me."

"A truce," he repeated. "I'm not a good drunk, usually not a bad drunk, but never a good drunk."

"Never touch me. Never touch me." She buried her face in her hands. "You promised you wouldn't hurt me. You promised you wouldn't let anyone hurt me."

Scott sucked at the air. He wasn't sure if he should put his arms around her to stop her shivering, but did anyway. "If I could take back what I did, I would, but I can't. We need each other, Helen. You want to find your sister. I want to find what was in the attaché case. We need each other."

"May's dead. Jessica's next. It's my fault."

He put her at arm's length. "Because of the money? How much does it take to sell out someone you love these days?"

"Enough to keep the Symphonic from bankruptcy for a long, long time."

"Who paid you?"

"'It's all very simple,' he told me. I give him the box. He gives me the money. I never see him again. Nothing ever happens."

"Tell me how I can find him?"

She heaved a gym bag onto the bed. "I want you to give it back to him. Tell him all I want is Jessica."

He looked her straight in the eye. "It's not that simple anymore. You want to see Jessica alive, right?"

She nodded soberly.

"You have to tell me everything. Everything. I want to know when the first time he approached you was. I want to know what he was wearing, what he looked like, what he smelled like, what he told you his name was. I want to know about every time you saw him after that first time. I want to know every word he told you. Whether it was raining or the sun was shining when you met. Everything."

Helen brought him back to last summer. The orchestra was having serious financial troubles. Their audience was shrinking. There wasn't enough money to pay the musicians for a third year in a row. A fifty percent pay cut was rejected by the musicians. They tried to raise funds, couldn't raise enough. And then he came with a suitcase full of hundred-dollar bills.

She unzipped the gym bag and handed him a stack of hundreds. "I just want Jessica back. That's all. Is that so terrible?"

He threw the wad of bills at her. "You don't know me well enough to buy me."

She appealed to him with her eyes. "Ten million. Ten million dollars."

"Go on," he told her.

The man didn't give her the money then, at least not all of it. He asked her how much she needed to keep the Symphonic running till December. She told him. He gave her the money, told her she owed him. She didn't see him again until January, when things were again desperate. A handful of musicians walked out, more were threatening to leave. They needed money. He took her out, wined and dined her and then attacked her. The next morning he was gone, but there was ten thousand dollars in the bed beside her.

In two weeks he came back, persuaded her that she was mistaken about the attack, told her that she was drunk at the time and didn't know what she was saying, told her she owed him and that she had to go with him right then. He took her to dinner at a fancy restaurant, got her drunk and then attacked her. It happened over and over and over, and always he left money. One day in early April, he came back with a suitcase full of money and told her how she could make him disappear forever.

She was trembling so violently that she couldn't go on. Scott held her, reassured her. This was the part he needed to hear. He pressed her to go on, to tell him everything. She did. Afterward, they sat on the bed for what seemed hours. His stomach was in knots. His hands were in fists. His fingernails were biting into his palms. Her tears were dripping down his back, but he hardly noticed as he gently rocked her back and forth, back and forth.

As evening set in, she sat in a chair and solemnly conducted Pachelbel's Canon in D. She said it was soothing. He said after four hours of listening to the music and watching her, it had surpassed annoying. In one end of the living room, there was a computer occupying a corner of a desk. He eyed it with a sense of longing. He asked her again, "No Newsnet access?"

She looked at him, didn't stop conducting. "No connection, no connection, no connection."

"Why would anyone have a computer and not have a connection?"

"Not my computer."

He tugged at his hair. "I have to get some fresh air."

She dropped her arms and ran to the stereo. "It's off. It's off. Don't leave."

"I'm just going to get some fresh air. Maybe I'll buy a newspaper. Is there a newsstand around here?"

"Mini-mart two blocks up, but it's late. They're out of papers by now."

Scott opened the door. Sunset was sprawled across the heavens; smog and ever-present humidity did nothing to dampen its beauty. It was a sunset Cynthia would've delighted in. He went to the railing and stared out over the glut of buildings to the distant horizon. Helen came up behind him. "Beautiful," she said. He walked away from her touch.

The mini-mart was three blocks up the street, not two, or maybe Scott went in the wrong direction but at the moment it didn't really matter. He wasn't daunted by the thickness of the Sunday *Tampa Tribune*. He bought the last one, a several-day-old *Wall Street Journal*, and a news rag that caught his eye. When he asked the man behind the counter if he still had yesterday's newspaper lying around somewhere, the man's face lit up with a smile. He produced a Friday and a Saturday edition. Scott bought both and a twenty-dollar phone card.

A few moments later, he was dialing Glen's number. Glen answered on the third ring. "How's Cynthia? Has she come around yet? What are the doctors saying?"

"Scott, you worry about the weather in Tampa. I'll worry about Cynthia for the both of us."

"And her condition?"

"She's getting stronger every day."

Scott closed his eyes, sighed.

Glen repeated, "Worry about the weather in Tampa."

"Is it going to rain?"

"I think there's a storm coming your way. Can you handle it?"

"A hurricane?"

"Could blow over in a day or two. Still, maybe you should stay indoors."

"I will." Scott hung up the phone, reached for his holster to reassure himself, found he wasn't wearing it. He looked around, picked up the newspapers and started back to Helen's apartment.

He walked as briskly as he could without running. He set the papers down at the base of the stairs, looked at them for a moment like he was parting with an old friend, then crept quietly up, one stair at a time. He stopped a few steps below the second floor landing. The door to the apartment was wide open. He could hear music coming from the stereo, but it wasn't Pachelbel.

He snaked up the last few stairs and into the apartment. The living room was empty. He smelled something faintly. Cigarette smoke. Helen didn't smoke, did she?

His gun was in the bedroom, somewhere. The question was how to get to it if someone was waiting for him within the shadowed apartment. He pulled at his lips as he considered his options, not surprised that the possibility of danger excited him.

Glen told him once that the thrill of the game was in his blood and for a long time he didn't know what Glen meant. One day, in a single instant, that changed. U.S. warplanes raced overhead. The city trembled as B-52s delivered their payloads. He hunkered down beside a wall that seemed to run forever along the banks of the Tigris and waited, waited just like he had outside the walls of Enieshkey and Serseng palaces in Amadiya, only things were different now. The push was on, the hunt was on, and he the hunter sought a more elusive quarry.

There was smoke then too, not faint but puissant and stinging as it rolled along the wall. He slipped into the bedroom, using the shadows as he moved. He groped along the floor beside the bed. He grinned as he touched soft leather and cold steel. He slipped the gun from the holster and was rising from his knees when he heard something not far off.

Abruptly, the bedroom light turned on. He squinted as he spun around, slipped his finger over the trigger and started to squeeze even before he saw what he was aiming it.

"No, Scott, no!" Helen screamed. She jumped in front of the woman who had turned on the light. "This is May. Scott, May. May, Scott. It's her apartment! Don't shoot! Please God don't shoot!"

He lowered the gun. Helen ran up to him and kissed him full on the mouth. Scott didn't shy away but it was only because of May. He whispered as she wrapped her arms around him and led him into the kitchen, "Knock it off."

Helen made coffee and put biscuits out. May watched, eyeing Scott without saying a word.

"Can I ask you a few questions, May? I need to know about Pattie."

May puffed on her cigarette, finished it, lit another. Scott swore a cloud was forming around her.

"Have you ever met Pattie?"

May didn't say anything.

Scott nodded to Helen. Helen said, "He's a friend, May. I vouch for him." Helen kissed him again, then sat down on his lap. "He's here to help. I asked him to."

"I really only met Pattie that once, at the airport."

"Go on." Scott sipped his coffee, wished it was something else and not only because the thin ceramic mug felt like it was burning his hand every time he touched it. May lit another cigarette, her fifth. Helen nibbled her thumbnail more intently.

May finally said, "It's mine and it isn't, really my ex-husband's. We're sort of trial and erroring it. Well, mostly erroring it right now if you know what I mean."

Scott said, "That's not what I asked. I asked you about Pattie. You said you met her at the airport once. Where did she fly in from?"

"Well, I'm trying to think. Sometimes it helps just to blab and then it just sort of comes in from the blue… See, now." May smiled. "One of those East Coast cities. You know, the big ones that start with a B that most of us folk down here don't rightly care about."

"Like Baltimore?"

"Baltimore, Boston, Boise. One of those."

Helen took May's hand. "Boise is in Idaho, dear."

May wrinkled her nose.

Scott reached for a biscuit and spilled his coffee in the process. Helen jumped off his lap, grabbed a handful of paper towel from a double-roll dispenser and was about to mop up the mess when May said, "No, that's the good stuff," as if she were talking about her best china.

Helen's face flushed red. Scott knew she was embarrassed for May but shouldn't have been. He also knew Helen thought he was angry, but he wasn't. He was starting to like May. Someone else might have thought her simple, but sometimes simple was refreshing. Helen put the paper towel back and slowly unrolled a few sheets from the other roller while May nodded her head. Scott took the paper towels from Helen and started cleaning up the mess.

Scott sat back down. "Tell me about Pattie."

"Pretty thing. Pretty eyes. Long black hair—well, used to be. She didn't like it that way, so one day Pattie up and chops it all off. Pattie was good for her though, real smart. Meant for each other but I guess that's in the past now."

"Did she ever talk about friends and family back home?"

"She's real quiet, you know. Most times."

"Her job. Did she ever talk about her job?"

"She flew first-class. Did I tell you that? Like a regular V.I.P. The type that brought my daddy to Boca Raton. It's not like it used to be. Nope, not no more. Getting sucked right into that giant cesspool in Miami."

Scott tensed again. Helen grabbed his arm and whispered in his ear, "She's having a rough time right now. Just leave her alone for a while."

"You two look good together," May said.

"I'm married."

May's eyes darted toward the bedroom. "How married?"

"I love my wife."

May sipped her coffee. "Too bad. You'd be good for each other."

Helen frowned and turned away.

"Back to Pattie," Scott said. "Was she going to fly in the weekend before last?"

"It was the first of January, right?"

"And?"

"It's a special day, you know. One year, one year. They met at some big conference in Miami last December. Some big to-do at one of those fancy hotels. Loves those fancy hotels. She'd find an excuse to spend the night in one just because she had a doctor's appointment and there was one a mile away. Surprised you don't know that by now."

"You're talking about Jessica, right?"

May rolled her eyes.

"This fancy hotel. Was it in Miami Beach, the Ritz-Carlton?"

"Like the cracker. That's the one. How'd you know?"

Scott eyed Helen who still wouldn't look at him. "Lucky guess. Does she always carry a lot of cash with her?"

May laughed like she was remembering a private joke that she kept hearing over and over. Helen got up and walked away. She went into the other room and turned on Pachelbel's Canon in D.

Scott said, "She paid for the room in cash, for a week in advance."

"I was her father's secretary for a while before he passed on, you know," May said, whispering now. "She came straight from the big college with that bee degree. You know B-E-E like in bumblebee. Anyway that's how I remember when I have to tell someone over the phone. 'Yes, she's certified,' I say. 'She's very good. The best, even better than her father.' That's a compliment."

Scott nodded. "And?"

"Well, just so you know. I've known her for a long, long time, you know. I was there all those years when no one else was. Anyway, she's the Queen of Credit. That's what I call her when she floats the bills from card to card to card. Last year she didn't come back for a week after that big to-do. Oh we had the police out looking last year. This year, I asked her, 'So you'll be back on Monday?' She laughs and says, 'Fred's in the Keys, right?' I nod. She says, 'Go visit him. Stay a few weeks.' So I go, only he's not there, he's here and now I'm here and he's not. We miss each other like that a lot sometimes."

"So Pattie paid for the room?"

"Well, probably. Always has money, that Pattie. That's partly why they would have been good for each other. Last year, she racked up ten thousand dollars during just that one week."

"Pattie?"

"No, silly. She was trying to impress Pattie, always. She likes to pretend like she has all the money in the world, but me and Pattie, we know it's an act. No, I didn't tell her and don't you tell that I told you either."

Scott's eyes glazed over for a moment, then he promised he wouldn't. He started thinking about credit cards, Jessica's credit cards and a paper trail all across Miami. "Thank you, May," he said, "You've been very helpful."

"Well, ain't you a dear," May said. She finished off her cigarette, went to get another one and found the pack was empty. As she started digging through her purse looking for a new pack, he went off in search of Helen.

Chapter 10

Miami, Florida
Monday, 10 January

It was a three-hour drive from Tampa to Alligator Alley along I-75. Helen asked why he wanted to take the tollway when I-41 would get them to Miami just fine and not that much later. It was the wee hours of a Monday morning and not a Monday afternoon. He agreed with her on that point, only that point. So the tollway was twelve bucks, big deal.

Helen said she remembered when it was only a buck fifty. Big deal. The point was that he could, and did, go from Naples to Andytown in an hour and not three.

He said smugly, "Miami Beach, two-fifteen in the a.m."

"Like we're going to do something at two-fifteen?" Helen had been in a sour mood ever since they left May's.

He took his foot off the accelerator. ""What did I do, what did I do that was so bad?"

"You acted like you were conducting an interrogation, that's what. Do you know how much that poor woman's been through?"

He looked away from the road for a moment and looked her straight in the eye. "What's this really about?"

"You know, don't you," Helen said glumly. "She told you didn't she, told you how much of a disappointment I was."

He came to a red light and stopped. "We're all disappointments to someone."

She started to reply. He cut her off, noticing the blue F-150 stopped in front of them and the black Excursion coming up from the rear. Something was out of place but before he could think about it anymore, the light turned green. The F-150 continued straight in the direction he was heading.

He changed his mind, turned right just to be on the safe side. There wasn't a lot of traffic this early in the morning and three cars coming to the same stop light, from the same direction, didn't feel right. As the Excursion turned right and the driver of the F-150 went into reverse, he yelled, "Buckle up…" just before he threw the shift into reverse, suddenly happy that he'd taken the upgrade offered at Tampa International but also wishing the car wasn't fire-engine red.

The back-end of the T-bird did a smooth 180. He stamped on the accelerator just as the Excursion sped past him. The driver of the F-150 was coming around at the same time, he swerved to miss him, ignoring the next red light as he raced away.

A second Excursion came into view. The driver swerved to block the street. Scott zigged and zagged to get around him. He swung around a corner, ignoring ONE WAY and NO TURN signs.

The F-150 was the only vehicle that could keep up at this point, but the other two drivers hadn't given up. He could see their headlights in the rearview mirror.

The F-150 was right on his tail. He shifted, stamped on the accelerator. The back-end fishtailed a bit but they'd surely make a clean getaway: A pickup truck couldn't outrun or outmaneuver a muscle car.

The T-bird topped out at 120. He was sure he could get more speed if the road leveled out but it was fast enough for now. The narrow one-way street made it seem like the buildings were closing in on them and Helen was already screaming, "Stop the car! Stop the car!"

He slammed on the brakes but not because she asked him to: The street was ending and a black SUV was parked in the T of the intersection. The dim streetlight offered just enough light to see armed men standing in front of the SUV.

He slowed down, planning to make a right turn but he was going too fast to maintain control of the car. The car spun through a half circle, the sliding back-end sent the gunmen running. As the left side of the T-bird slammed into the SUV, the driver-side window shattered.

He pulled Helen down in the seat just before he raced off, expecting the gunmen to open fire but they didn't. He raced down several streets, turning randomly. At an on-ramp to the interstate, he jammed on the brakes and the T-bird skidded to a halt. "You okay?" he asked.

Helen bobbed her head, absently saying, "You?"

Scott waited, watching the rearview mirror. "Nothing a few stitches won't fix." He leaned over, turned his left shoulder to her. "You any good with a needle and thread?"

Seeing the blood and glass brought Helen back to reality. She unwrapped her arms from around her shoulders, stopped shaking. "You should see a doctor."

He shifted, accelerated, started onto the interstate. He took the next exit, came back around to the Ritz-Carlton. He didn't pull up front. Instead, he went around back. "Switch places with me," he told her.

She furrowed her brow but did as he asked.

As he came around the car, he opened the trunk. His garment bag had a field kit. He tossed it to Helen. "Always pays to be prepared."

"Well just what do you want me to do with this?" She took a closer look at his arm, started pulling out the glass shards. "You need stitches."

He reached over with his right hand, pushed in the lighter, waited. "Get the needle and thread."

"You want me to stitch you up. Here?"

"Here."

"I'm liable to stitch you up crooked."

"Just like conducting, Helen, only use small, deliberate strokes. There's a bottle under the driver's seat."

"You don't need a drink," she shot back. "Sober or drunk the result will be the same."

"Not for me, for the shoulder. Douse the shoulder. Bourbon's a pretty good antiseptic, trust me."

She poured the booze on the shoulder, sterilized the needle with the cigarette lighter and went to work. She put in twelve stitches along the jagged gash. He sat still, unflinching when the needle went in, and just as steady when the thread was pulled tight and knotted.

Afterward, she helped him put on a clean shirt and a light jacket. A few minutes later he drove the T-bird around to the front of the Ritz-Carlton.

He unlocked the trunk for the porter, gave the car keys and an Abraham Lincoln to a kid who looked barely sixteen, then escorted her into the hotel. They both ignored questions about the broken window and the battered fenders.

Following Scott's nod, Helen went to the counter. She asked if they could check back in to Room 908. The room was available.

Not long afterward, Scott found himself eyeballing the single king-size bed in Room 908. Helen went into the bathroom to freshen up. He removed his jacket and shoes, then claimed the left side of the bed.

Helen emerged from the bathroom a few minutes later. She was naked. No surprise. He ignored her and closed his eyes.

She said, "Are you going to sleep with that thing strapped around your shoulder?"

"The gun stays where it is. Turn off the light."

"It could get in the way."

"Nothing's going to happen, Helen."

She turned off the light, climbed in bed and started blowing in his ear. "Even now?"

"Go to sleep." He rolled onto his side.

"I can't sleep." She turned the light back on.

He rolled onto his back, stared at her.

She turned onto her side facing him. She said softly, "Who did you disappoint?"

Scott was quiet. He tried not to let himself feel anything.

She repeated, "Who did you disappoint?"

"My father wanted me to be a doctor. My mother wanted me to be a lawyer. But I sort of went into the family business instead."

"Would you hate me forever if I disappointed you, like you hate them for making you something you're not?"

"I don't hate my parents, and nobody made me what I am. I made me what I am."

"That's not the truth, I see it behind your eyes. May saw it. I see it. That's why she said we'd be good together. She's never wrong."

"There are things I choose not to remember because I don't want to." He reached over her and shut off the table lamp. "Get some sleep."

When he awoke it was almost noon and he thought the world had surely ended. Beside him, Helen was still sleeping. He went to the window and drew back the drapes. As bright sunshine bathed the room, Helen moaned and pulled a pillow over her head. He went into the bathroom and took a shower. Soap and hot water tore away the stiffness of a long and fitful sleep. He was careful not to get the bandaged shoulder wet but the bandage got soaked anyway.

He was in the midst of washing that spot in the middle of his back that he could never quite reach when he heard the bathroom door open. Helen folded back the shower curtain. He expected her to step into the shower with him. Instead, she just poked her head in and said, "The phone's ringing. Should I answer it?"

He looked at her. She smiled. "You couldn't have said that from over there?"

"And miss this?" She smiled again. "Should I answer it or not?"

"Answer it if that's what you want to do."

"That's not what I want to do, but I'll do it."

He soaped up his underarms, rinsed the conditioner out of his hair, then let the hot water soothe him for a moment more before getting out of the shower. If there was one thing he would remember about the Ritz-Carlton, it would be their towels: soft and plush. His garment bag was in the closet. He took out a clean pair of slacks, a matching jacket, and a button-down cotton shirt. No tie, he felt constrained in a tie, and only wore one when it was a necessity.

He had his shirt halfway buttoned when he remembered his shoulder and the bandages that needed to be changed. "Helen?" he called out, "Can you help me with this?"

There was no answer. He took the field kit out of the bag and set about cutting gauze and taping it over the wound.

He finished buttoning up the cotton shirt in front of the bathroom mirror and went to find his boots. He noticed the hotel room door was ajar. The TV was on, so he presumed Helen was watching it. He called out, "Helen?"

He walked toward the blaring TV. "Helen?"

The room was empty. The phone rang. Scott snatched it up. "Helen, where are you?"

"Are you watching the TV?"

"Who is this?"

"Are you watching the TV?"

He turned toward the TV. "Who is this?"

The phone went dead. He noticed this only vaguely as he stared at the TV. The twelve o'clock news was on. He sat down on the edge of the bed. His stomach muscles bunched up in knots.

"Tampa firefighters have been battling this four-alarm fire since dawn. Local residents say there was an explosion around 5 a.m., what appears to be a gas explosion, and that the building went up in a huge fireball that threatened to consume its neighbors. The neighboring apartment buildings were evacuated within minutes, but the fire here at Emerald Grove burned so hot and so quick firefighters are not sure if anyone survived. This is Tina—"

Scott clicked off the TV, his thoughts turned to Helen. He slipped on his boots as he stumbled to the elevator. When the elevator opened on the first floor, he raced through the lobby to the street. The street was a moving mass of humanity. He closed his eyes for an instant to recall what Helen wore the day before, which he hoped she was wearing now—a baggy, yellow sun dress. He stared up and down the street. Baggy, yellow sun dress. Baggy, yellow sun dress.

He ran back to the hotel lobby, went to the front desk. "Did anyone see a woman with long black hair, wearing a yellow sun dress?"

One of the clerks shrugged. Another recommended he try the pool area or the beach. He went out to the pool and the beach, but didn't find Helen. He went back to the room thinking she might have returned there. The room was just as he left it. His mind started working. The keys, the car keys. Where were they? They weren't in his pocket. They weren't on the nightstand.

He pulled at his hair and shouted at the walls, but it didn't help. He searched the room in case the keys dropped out of his pocket. Helen's purse was on the table. The gym bag full of money was tossed casually in the closet right where the porter left it. Helen's overnight bag was beside the bed. Only the car keys were missing.

He called down to the front desk, told them he was checking out and asked if they would get the bill ready and send up a porter. He hung up the phone and closed his eyes as he tried to think. If he were Helen, where would he go? Would she drive back to Tampa? Not likely, not Helen. Would she go home? Would she go back to Boca Raton? Maybe, if she thought Jessica might be there.

He rented another car. Hertz delivered it to the Ritz-Carlton. It wasn't rush hour, so it was only a forty-minute drive to Boca Raton, and in less than an hour, he was parking around the corner from J. Wellmen & Associates. He looked for the red T-bird he rented in Tampa, but didn't see it.

The front door of the office was closed and locked. He walked around to the back door. He took a set of lock picks out of his inside jacket pocket, not bothered by the fact that it was broad daylight and the little side street wasn't deserted. He opened the door, glanced back over his shoulder, then entered.

His eyes went wide as he closed the door behind him. The reception area was a mess. The desk was on its side. The couch was ripped apart. One of the closet doors was off its hinges. He raced into the back room. The floor of the room was wall-to-wall gizmos before but now it was clean swept, as if someone went over it inch by inch with a magnifying glass. The little desk in the far corner of the room was the same way, stripped bare—or was it?

He saw something on the desktop. Papers maybe. No, a note. A note from Helen.

He started reading:

Scott,

Made a mess of things, didn't I? Don't hate me. I didn't have a choice. Don't look for me. You won't find me. No one will find me ever again. No one will hurt me ever again.

I wanted to help you. You have to know that, but I couldn't. Do you see now what happens when I say things I shouldn't? I have something he wants. He has something I want. Do you understand?

Probably not. Well, you don't need to. I left something for you, Scott. You're my ace in the hole. Check your beige jacket.

Helen of Troy

Scott ran back to the car, unzipped the garment bag and took out his beige sports coat. He worked his way through the pockets one at a time, carefully, because he wasn't sure what he would find. In the inside left breast pocket, he found three pieces of folded-up paper. He unfolded them. They read:

Thursday, December 9
XWEH

Friday, December 10
Deliver PT 2:00

Saturday, December 11
Airport 8:30

These were the missing days from the desk calendar. In a few hours, Scott would realize how valuable these clues were, but right now he was pissed off and more than ready to tear his hair out. *Don't hate me.* What the hell did that mean? If Helen wanted to help him, she should've stayed, should've told him everything a long time ago.

He leaned over, put his head against the wall. More than anything he wanted to be home with Cynthia but he no longer felt worthy of her love. He'd done things that he swore he'd never do with another woman. It didn't matter that he was coerced or drugged, what mattered was that deep down he enjoyed Helen's games.

He was sick. Sick. There was no other explanation.

Chapter 11

Miami, Florida
Tuesday, 11 January

Scott drove three blocks to the 7-11 down the street from J. Wellmen & Associates. Someone was on the pay phone. He glanced at his watch to check the time and waited in the car until the phone became available. Glen would still be at the office in DC. He dialed the office number. Someone answered. He said, "Hello."

There was silence on the other end of the line for a long time. He knew someone was there because he heard breathing, then finally Glen replied, "Clear blue sky."

He told Glen about finding the missing calendar pages, the two cryptic messages and the reference to the airport, but didn't say how they came into his possession. "Do you think the boys in Analysis can make something of that?"

"You'll know when I know."

"How long will the Apollo search take?"

"It'll take some time. I'll make sure they make a clean sweep. Wellmen or Johnson—Johnson, right?"

"Johnson, yes."

"We'll find it if it's there. Give me a call back in a few hours."

"I need some help with a credit card search on Jessica and Helen. All purchases in the last few—"

"Get to a fax. You'll have everything you need."

"I'm outside a 7-11, I'll get their Q-fax number—"

"Scott, there's one thing I have to ask. Is your guest still with you?"

He was suddenly glad he wasn't on a video phone. "In the car, why?"

"Good. Get me that fax number."

He switched the phone to his right ear. "How is Cynthia?"

"Stronger. Her father has made arrangements for private nurses. He wants her home and not in a sterile hospital. Says confidently the smell of her room, the house, will bring her back. I believe him. The doctors say there's no explanation as to why she hasn't come out of the coma."

"I'm going to get this bastard, Glen, if it's the last thing I ever do." He hung up the phone.

Ten minutes after he called Glen back and gave him the fax number, the Q-fax at the 7-11 came to life. Two hot dogs and a

Big Gulp later, a thirty-page fax had finally finished printing. It was Jessica's credit purchase history for the last ninety days. A minute later, the fax came to life again, this time it printed a single page containing Helen's purchase history for the same period.

After poring through Jessica's purchases looking for purchase patterns, Scott decided to focus. He spent two days piecing together what he was sure was the last month of Jessica's life, from the purchase of a handgun on the eleventh of November to the final purchase of two peach cobblers on the first of December. It seemed her life lay on the motel bed, written on little scraps of paper organized by day and week.

Jessica had sixteen major credit cards, eight department store cards, and three gas cards. She charged everything from a pack of gum to an eighteen-hundred-dollar designer dress. She ate lunch at Alfredo's every Thursday. Four bills for $32.08.

He went to Alfredo's. "I'm Ms. Wellmen's accountant. I need to finalize the year end. Was that a party of two—business lunch?" "No, that was a party of one." "J. Wellmen, right?" "Yes, spaghetti and marinara. Extra sauce. Don't deliver the espresso until the plate is gone." "Are you sure?" "Yes, I'm sure. No cream. No sugar. Ten-dollar tip. Wellmen."

Through other purchases, Scott followed Jessica up the coast on two weekend getaways. Three fill-ups. A stop for supper in Palm Bay. A breakfast, a lunch, and a supper at a tiny restaurant on the outskirts of Summer Haven. Two fill-ups. A stop for brunch in Palm Bay.

On Fridays, if she was melancholy, she bought a Big Gulp and a box of Twinkies, charged it to Visa Platinum. Ed from the

7-11 attested to the fact that she never ate it. Rather, she purchased it, Ed consumed and Jessica watched. They talked until his shift ended. Never anything more than the weather, the news or his family. Jessica mostly listened while Ed told her about his three daughters, five sons and eighteen grandchildren. Jessica was a good listener, or at least that's what Ed said.

Every day. The pattern of every day of her life was before his eyes. On Wednesday afternoons, twice a month, she went to Piedro's. She got her hair done and sometimes a manicure. She spent an average of fifty-two dollars a week on groceries, which she charged to a card that she didn't use for anything else. She charged gas at Texaco, except for her weekend trips. Those charges went to Chevron.

Every day. Every day of her life was before his eyes.

On the other hand, Helen had one credit card, MasterCard. Not platinum, not gold, just a plain old ordinary credit card with a five-hundred-dollar limit. In December, she had used the card only once: A charge to T & T Towing when her jalopy broke down. The car was still at the garage where the tow truck left it. Tom, the owner of the garage, told Scott, "You can get the car back if you pay the repair bill." "How much is it?" "Twenty-six hundred." "Dollars?" "Yep, repairs ain't cheap, you know." The car in Scott's estimation was barely worth its weight in scrap metal.

Scott asked, "Can I check the car? I think my wife left some things in the back seat." The owner told him, "Sure, when you pay the twenty-six hundred you can do whatever you want." "Did she ask for these repairs?" "Sure, got it right here in writing." It was a note scratched on a cocktail napkin:

Fix this piece of shit car when you get a chance. Call me if it's under a million. 555-8125.

Helen

Scott told Tom, "Enjoy your investment," and slipped the cocktail napkin into his pocket when old Tom wasn't looking.

So now after a second long day of running around Southeast Florida, he was back to the scraps of paper organized neatly on a cheap motel bed. Helen, the single piece of paper and a napkin on the pillow. Jessica, the meticulously separated heaps occupying the rest of the bed.

He was staring at the cocktail napkin from Pete's Bar & Grill when he thought of Glen—Glen, who he hadn't called in two days. He would've called Glen right then if it wasn't for the phone number Helen had scrawled on the napkin. It wasn't the number to Helen's apartment, Jessica's apartment or either of Jessica's office phones. Whose phone number was it? And why did it catch his eye now when he had looked at it a dozen times?

The number was to a cellular phone. The phone belonged to Jessica Wellmen and the phone bill was sixty days past due, so the phone company had disconnected service. He found that out in two phone calls and fifteen minutes. He offered, "I'll pay the bill if you'll send me an audit of calls for the last three months. How much is owed?" "Six-hundred eighteen dollars and fifty-three cents." "Six hundred dollars? That's outrageous. There has to be a mistake. How long will it take to get the phone audit? "Seven to ten business days." "Seven to ten days? Are you kidding me? Who do I have to talk to to get that now?" "You can talk to my supervisor but it ain't going to do you no good."

On a hunch Scott decided to drive out to Pete's Bar & Grill. He needed to wind down and perhaps he could find someone there who knew Helen and Jessica. Pete's Bar & Grill was in West Palm Beach, on the beach. The music was a blend of calypso that wasn't really reggae. The crowd, mostly tourists. And Pete was a permanent fixture behind the bar. Pete was a gator, one big, stuffed alligator.

After two Mai Tais, nonalcoholic, he showed the picture of Jessica and Helen to the bartender. "Seen either of them?"

The bartender continued mixing a drink and didn't look in Scott's direction. "Not that many regulars, not a local hangout."

"You didn't look at the picture."

"I don't need to."

Scott edged an Andrew Jackson across the bar.

The bartender didn't take the money, but did glance at the picture. "Everyone's looking for a pretty lady tonight. I see lots of pretty ladies."

Scott pushed the picture and his glass across the bar. "Take a closer look. I'm not a cop. I'm a friend."

"Isn't everyone… Here's your drink. My recommendation is drink it and leave."

Scott put the picture into his pocket. "How's the food here?"

"Go upstairs and find out, I'm not the cook."

Scott registered the sudden chill, took his drink and filtered into the crowd. It was nearly ten. The band was starting to play louder. The dance floor had expanded and moved toward the sand. The tourists were swaying and bobbing their heads. For a

Friday night, Pete's was hopping.

He didn't plan on leaving right away. He wanted to watch the bartender for a while. The bartender had seemed agitated and protective, especially if Helen and Jessica were just another pair of pretty ladies. And if that were the case, why didn't he take the twenty?

He moved out to the shadowed beach and leaned against a palm tree. The bar was visible only intermittently through the gyrating crowd. He found the beat of the music strangely piquant. The lyrics didn't seem to make much sense. The lead singer was no Garth Brooks. But he thought maybe that was the point.

He listened and watched. The hours slipped away. Slowly the crowd thinned out. The music got quieter. Eventually, all that was left of the mammoth array of cars that had been lining the beach and filling the parking lot were a handful of vehicles belonging to the employees of Pete's Bar & Grill, and Scott's rented convertible.

The bartender seemed to be finished washing glasses. Scott stood and wiped the sand off his buttocks, but didn't go toward the bar. Two bouncers and most of the band were now occupying the stools along the bar. He decided to make his way to the parking lot and his car. There he'd wait for the bartender.

Midway up the sandy hill from the beach, he got a clear view of the vehicles near the lot. Only five now. A panel van. A pickup. His convertible, and two others. As he walked into the lot, he thought maybe there was a sixth car parked behind the panel van. And then as he moved closer, he knew there was no maybe about it. Even in the poor lighting of the lot, he could see the color of the car was red. It was a red T-bird, and not just any red T-bird. It was the smashed-up red T-bird he had rented in Tampa.

The car was locked and unoccupied, but that didn't bother him. He knew in that moment that Helen had been here and he was making headway.

He went around to the driver's side door, reached through the broken window and unlocked the door. Unfortunately, other than a crumpled bag from McDonald's, the car didn't offer many clues. The mileage on the car, 12076, was the biggest clue to where Helen had been. He closed his eyes and tried to picture the original mileage.

Remembering the rental car paperwork in the glove box, he found what he needed. The original mileage before he left Tampa International was 11551. Almost three hundred miles to Miami Beach, a trip to Boca Raton, a trip to West Palm Beach—about a hundred and fifty miles unaccounted for.

There was a trunk release in the glove box. He pushed it, heard a click. The trunk slowly opened. He was almost afraid of what he might find but checked anyway. He grinned, and in a way was pleased, when he looked into the trunk and found it was empty.

He went back to his car, which was parked along the road adjacent to the lot. While he waited for the bartender, he got out the Florida state map and drew three lines. One seventy-five miles north of West Palm Beach, one midway along the Florida Keys, and the last one at Fort Myers.

He searched with his hands across the map, city by city, working east, south, then north. Fort Myers was a long way off, and seventy-five miles even by the best of routes left him in the middle of nowhere. The same was true about the Keys: Key Largo wasn't that far, Marathon was too far. He worked his way north from West Palm Beach and finally came to Palm Bay. Palm Bay was one of Jessica's stops on her weekenders.

Maybe Jessica had done more than eat in Palm Bay? Maybe there was a connection to Helen? Maybe Helen believed Jessica might have gone off on one of her weekend jaunts? He thought about this, but didn't have time to dwell on it. He heard voices, then saw shadows mounting the hill to the lot. He slipped down in the convertible's front seat. The voices came closer and closer.

He twisted the rearview mirror so he could watch them get in their vehicles. The bartender got into the pickup by himself. The members of the band piled into the panel van and the two bouncers got in separate cars.

The pickup was the last to leave the lot. He waited to follow, but as the pickup started past him, the driver hit the brakes and wheeled in front of the convertible. The bartender emerged from the pickup wielding a baseball bat.

He yelled, "Come on, you S.O.B.! You like to hit women, try me on for size!"

Scott stepped out of the car. A moment later the panel van and the two other cars returned. The bartender grinned and slapped the baseball bat against his hand.

Scott raised his arms with open hands and circled as the bartender circled. "This is a mistake. I'm a friend of Helen's. I'm trying to find her."

"Well, she don't want to be found, now does she?"

In a moment, it was eight against one. He put his back against the convertible, took a deep breath. He could have pulled out his guns and ground this to a quick standstill, but he didn't. He waited.

He took another deep breath, told himself to remain calm, and more importantly, to look calm. He could put a bullet in each one of them, but would that help anything?

He said, "You have me mistaken with someone else. All I want to know is where she is?"

"She doesn't want to be found," yelled the bartender as he took a swing at Scott with the baseball bat.

Scott jumped back to get out of the way. "When was she here?"

"No business of yours."

They edged closer, closing Scott in a tight circle. The two bouncers had baseball bats like the bartender. One of the band members had a tire iron.

It was about to get ugly. Scott reached back and pulled out the gun casually, as if he was taking a cigarette out of a pack. He said calmly, "Is she worth dying for?"

The bouncers and the bartender came in swinging. Scott bobbed and weaved but held back from putting a bullet in one of them. Irritated when a bat buzzed his ear, he fired a shot. The bullet whooshed by one of the bouncers and broke out a window in the panel van.

The shot and the breaking glass got their attention. They stopped advancing, held their ground. The driver of the van was saying, "Not my van, not my van."

Scott reached down slowly with his free hand and took the .22 Beretta out of his boot. It evened the odds and helped him to keep a cool exterior. He glared at the bartender, said again, "Is she worth dying for?"

The van driver started edging away. He was mumbling, "Me no play that game, me no play that game," as if it were the lyrics to one of his songs.

Scott smiled at his right hand then his left. "Belgium and Italy. Ever been there? Old Pietro Beretta did a good thing here, don't you think? Not as much power as this—" He brandished the Browning as if it were a prize and cocked the hammer back on the Beretta. "But does it matter at point-blank range?"

He heard the panel van's engine start. The band members backed out one by one. The bouncers edged back to their cars and waited. Then it was only Scott and the bartender.

But just when he thought things were turning in his favor, the van driver stomped on the gas and the van lurched forward, right at Scott and the bartender. They both had to dive out of the way to avoid being hit. Missing the target, the driver plowed into the T-bird, but that didn't stop him. He put the van in reverse, gunned it again.

Scott shot out one of the rear tires just before he jumped out of the way, rolling in the sand. When the van passed him, he fired two shots, one hitting a front tire. The driver got out of the van and started kicking the tire just as the bartender came back in with the baseball bat. The aluminum bat careened off the side of the van as Scott ducked. Scott slapped the side of the bartender's head with the butt end of the Beretta.

The bartender went down. He put the Beretta to the side of the man's head, swept the Browning in a wide arc to keep the bouncers and their bats away. "Back off!" he shouted. "Back off!"

He turned back to the bartender and said coldly, "What's

your name? If I'm going to kill a man, I like to know his name."

"Screw you!"

He went to rap the bartender's head again with the butt end of the Beretta but stopped short. "Ten seconds and I pull the trigger. Look, all I'm asking for right now is your name."

One of the band members shouted, "I'm on the phone to 9-1-1. West Palm Beach P.D. is on the way, you asshole!"

Scott glanced in the direction the voice came from, still brandishing the Browning, and then looked back down at the bartender. "I'm not the one hurting Helen. I'm a friend, and I think she needs me right now more than you know. Your name?"

The bartender stuttered out his name. "Terr-ill. Terrill Johnson."

Scott started to respond, stopped. "As in Jessica Johnson?"

"As in brother."

Scott took a step back. They stared each other down for a moment. Scott didn't say anything. Terrill didn't say anything. Finally Scott said, "Where is Helen?"

"I wish I knew."

"And Jessica?"

Terrill repeated, "I wish I knew."

"What's in Palm Bay?"

"My mother, you asshole!"

Scott didn't have time to ask any more questions. He heard sirens off in the distance.

Terrill said, "They're going to lock you up for a long time, you sick son of a bitch."

Scott glared at Terrill as he backed away. The convertible top was down; he jumped in without opening the door. He was pulling away when he saw the first squad car coming over the hill. He kept going, didn't look back.

The pieces were starting to fall into place. This was good.

Chapter 12

Palm Bay, Florida
Saturday, 15 January

Mom Johnson lived in a retirement community that was a few miles outside Palm Bay. She was a pleasant woman in her sixties with the light of youth still in her eyes. Her hair was a rusted blonde that flowed to her shoulders. Her face was wrinkled in a pleasant way. And she was as strikingly beautiful as her daughters, yet this came from a delicate balance of refinement and youthful mannerisms, and not from the beauty of the flesh.

Behind her eyes she hid the pain of a hard life, Scott grasped at hints of this in her words as she walked him through the family photo albums and as he asked questions about Jessica and Helen.

"Did Helen say where she was going?"

"Helen and I aren't exactly conversant. On her rare visits, she doesn't tell and I don't ask." Mom Johnson touched a hand to her mouth and wavered her head. "Oh, would you look at this, my little seraph going to the prom."

Scott admired the picture of Jessica *and* Helen. Mom Johnson rocked back and forth.

"Harry always liked Summer Haven, you know. Sure he and Jessica had their differences, but she always was a daddy's girl. She visits him every couple of weeks. And Helen, well, she visits every now and again when she's in trouble."

"Harry?"

"My husband, Harry."

"Harry Johnson?" Scott paused to try to think of how to phrase the question correctly. "I thought he passed away?"

"Naw, Harry's up at Meadow Park. He likes it up there, told you he always liked Summer Haven. If you're looking for Jessica, you'll find her there. That's for sure." Mom Johnson turned to the next page of the album, put her hand to her mouth again. "Would you look at that? Graduation. Jessica was straight A's, valedictorian. I bet you didn't know that."

"—and Helen?"

"Well, Helen was Helen."

"Is there an address in Summer Haven? That would help out a lot."

"Naw, when you get to Summer Haven, ask someone how to get to Meadow Park. They'll tell you. I haven't been up there in years. Jessica didn't come last weekend, you know. I miss my little seraph. You see her, you tell her."

It was late in the afternoon when he left Mrs. Johnson's home. He had soaked up as much about Helen and Jessica as he possibly could. He wanted to get a good feel for their backgrounds and Mrs. Johnson provided that and more. The sisters had grown up in a stable home. No hints of violence. The family, once affluent, lost nearly everything on Black Monday and what they didn't lose, the banks foreclosed on. Jessica was, as far as her mother was concerned, forever polite, always outgoing and always with a handsome man on her arm. Helen was always unusual and introverted, and as of late, what her mother termed as "quaint like Uncle Howard." And Uncle Howard was in a "sanitarium" upstate.

It would take about three hours to drive to Summer Haven. Scott was famished. He hadn't eaten since breakfast, discounting the cookies and milk Mrs. Johnson had given him and he had obligingly eaten. He stopped at a 7-11 to fill up the car, and afterward, he bought two frozen burritos and a Big Gulp. He set the timer on a tiny microwave next to the counter to seven minutes and went to make a phone call. He didn't know why, but suddenly he remembered Glen. Glen who he hadn't called since Tuesday.

He dialed the office first, just in case Glen was still there. He let the phone ring while he stared at the cars racing up and down Palm Bay Road. Then for a moment, he closed his eyes and saw the face that had been gnawing at the back of his mind for days. Every time he closed his eyes, every time, he saw her face and all because of a single instant when he had recalled everything but her face.

The phone ringing in his ear brought him back. He hung up

and dialed Glen's home number. The phone rang and rang, but no one picked it up. He slammed the phone down and went back into the 7-11 for his burritos.

The sun was setting when he arrived in Summer Haven. He stopped at a gas station and asked for directions to Meadow Park. The clerk looked at him strangely, then told him, "Up the road a ways, when you see the headstones, you're looking at Meadow Park."

"A cemetery?"

"Meadow Park, right?"

He didn't answer. He got back into his convertible and drove away. Meadow Park was right up the road. If he had just kept going without stopping at the gas station, he probably would've seen it but never would've turned in. He was suddenly curious. Jessica drove all the way up from Boca Rotan every two weeks to visit a cemetery? There had to be something more.

Meadow Park was a small cemetery with a panoramic view of the Atlantic Ocean. There was a groundskeeper near the gate. He was putting the finishing touches on a row of hedges. As Scott drove in, he flagged Scott down. "We close her up at sunset."

"I'll only be a few minutes, less if you can help me."

"No need to hurry, people's always in a rush, and that's how they end up here."

Scott offered a friendly smile. "I'm looking for Harry Johnson's plot."

"You looking for Harry Johnson?"

Scott said, "Yes." The groundskeeper gave him directions and told him he'd keep the gate open until he returned. Harry Johnson's grave was before the third bend in the road, atop the second hill, and under a great oak tree, provided he made a right-hand turn where the groundskeeper told him to, which he did.

He parked along the side of the road and climbed to the top of the hill. Right under the boughs of the great oak tree was Harry Johnson's tombstone. The plots on either side of him were unoccupied, and there were fresh flowers on the grave.

He stared out at the ocean for a moment. The view under the darkening sky was breathtaking, even more so toward sunset. He kneeled down and examined the beautiful collection of summer flowers—fresh-cut summer flowers and not a hint of wilting. He stayed only long enough to focus his thoughts on the two sisters. Helen and Jessica came to Summer Haven to see more than a grave, had to.

He thought about Jessica's credit card bills and the weekend trips up the coast. Three fill-ups. A stop for supper in Palm Bay. A breakfast, a lunch, and a supper at a tiny restaurant on the outskirts of Summer Haven. Two fill-ups. A stop for brunch in Palm Bay. What was missing?

He grinned toothily as May's words echoed in his mind. "Jessica loves those fancy hotels. She'd find an excuse to spend the night in one just because she had a doctor's appointment and there was one a mile away."

Hotel bills. No hotel bills.

Scott got in his car and drove back to the front gate. The groundskeeper was waiting for him. Scott stopped to thank him and ask if he'd seen anyone bring flowers to Harry's grave today.

"Speed limit's five miles-per-hour for a reason."

"I didn't know—"

"It's posted."

"I'm awful sorry. The grounds are beautiful. Do you do all the work yourself?"

"Me and my boy."

"Then you see just about everyone coming and going?" He took out the picture of Helen and Jessica.

"I like to say hello to most folks. Try to be friendly, you know."

"Did you see who brought the flowers to Harry's grave today? They were awful pretty."

"One of his daughters, I suspect."

Scott showed him the picture, pointed to Helen. "Was she here today?"

"I don't need to look at that. They're both real private types, so I stay out of their way. The youngest, she sits up there for hours sometimes watching the water. The other one, well I don't see her much, but I reckon that was her this morning."

"Do you remember the time?"

"Don't keep a watch, don't want to know. Either the sun's up or it isn't."

"When was the last time you saw Jessica Johnson?"

The groundskeeper removed his cap and scratched his head. "Don't rightly recall, been a while."

"Do the Johnsons have relatives in Summer Haven?"

"You ask a lot of questions, you with the police?"

"No, just thought I might find Helen up here, that's all." Scott reached into the back seat and grabbed Helen's purse. "We're kind of seeing each other, and well, she left in a huff. Her purse. I really would've liked to return it to her and maybe apologize too."

"Well young man—" No one had called Scott "young man" in years. "—Either you're seeing her or you aren't, there's no kind of about it. Check the Orange Tree, I'm headed there for supper myself."

"That was on the left a ways back?"

"I imagine it was."

The Orange Tree was the restaurant Jessica frequented when she visited Summer Haven. It was a Mom and Pop place where he was sure he'd get a good meal, but not the sort of place that would fulfill Mom and Pop's American dream. The ancient, water-stained "For Sale By Owner" sign in the front window attested to this.

He sat at the front counter and ordered fried chicken. The meal came with soup, salad and a choice of side dish. He said he'd like mashed potatoes and gravy. He was the restaurant's sole occupant, so he figured his rumbling stomach would be filled in a matter of minutes. This was not the case, and he imagined he could've driven back to the KFC in Miami Beach faster. Still, the spicy fried chicken, a whole chicken, and mashed potatoes made from real potatoes were as good as he expected and certainly worth the wait.

Scott was licking his fingers when the groundskeeper and a youngster, probably his son, came into the restaurant. He waved. Scott waved back. The father and son took a table next to a window. As Scott turned back to his plate, he heard the door open and close. He turned his head toward the door. His eyes went wide and despite the urge to jump from his seat, he remained seated. He looked down at the plate and leaned on his left hand in an attempt to hide his face.

He heard heels pass by the counter, a chair draw back. He watched out of the corner of his eye and said casually, "Keneke Kawena, Honolulu Police Department. How's it going? Still playing detective I see."

Ken bashed his knees on the table as he jumped up. "This isn't what you're thinking."

"Maybe not, but you might as well join me."

Ken took a few uneasy steps toward Scott. "I'm not following you, if that's what you're thinking."

Scott lied. "That's not what I was thinking at all."

Ken took a stool next to Scott. "The truth is I was following you. I figured you might have given me the slip when you didn't come out, so I decided to come in."

"Bad choice." Scott sipped his Coca-Cola, asked the man behind the counter if he'd bring another. "How long you been following me?"

"Since I saw you'd returned to the hotel, since Wednesday night."

Scott raised an eyebrow and laughed into his Coca-Cola. He didn't say that he had returned to the hotel on Monday. Instead he said, "Since Wednesday night, the whole time, no shit?"

"Yes."

"Well, you were doing a bang-up job until a few minutes ago." Scott's voice changed, the tone became less friendly. "Why you following me, Ken, and don't test my patience?"

"I work in the fraud division, remember?"

Scott sighed. "How could I forget? And I suppose you're going to tell me about the cuckoo's egg now?"

"It's a book," Ken said, as if that would illuminate everything.

The man behind the counter hadn't brought Scott's bill yet. Scott took out his wallet and smiled at him. When the man didn't come over, Scott asked, "Will twenty dollars settle it?"

"Chicken's eight ninety-five, dollar-fifty for two sodas, tax, tip for my wife—twelve dollars outta cover it."

Scott gave the man a Hamilton and two Lincolns, and slipped an Andrew Jackson under the plate. Scott grabbed a clean paper napkin, took out a pen and thought for a moment about what phone number to write down. Ken watched him curiously. Scott wrote his Baltimore phone number on the napkin and folded it in half. Ken waited expectantly, but Scott stood and walked over to the groundskeeper. "You see Helen or Jessica, please give this to them. Tell them they can call day or night."

The groundskeeper said he would. Scott left the restaurant. Ken followed. Scott walked away from the lights of the restaurant, away from the street lights, and into the darkness of the parking lot. He heard footsteps not far behind and walked a little faster. Abruptly, he stopped, whirled about and drew his gun. Ken nearly walked into him. Scott grabbed him by the shirt, stuck his gun in Ken's ear, and cocked the hammer back.

"You have exactly five seconds to tell me who you really are, and your stupid act isn't going to work anymore, so don't try it."

"Keneke Kawena—"

"Drop the act."

"It's the truth. Keneke Kawena is the name on my birth certificate. I work for HPD in the fraud division. I was investigating an unauthorized user on the Apollo res. system, not the sort of thing we usually do, but fraud is fraud. No matter if it takes place in the ether or on the streets, fraud is fraud, and computer fraud is what I like to do."

Scott removed the gun from Ken's ear. "Keep talking."

"The Information Highway isn't all miracles, you know. The number of hijackers in the ether grows exponentially every year, and someone has to track them down."

"And?"

"It's what I do best. Unauthorized access simply isn't enough. I track down unauthorized users who commit computer fraud. In the case of fraud, we can make a case. There's two of us who handle computer fraud. We get no support from anyone and the department spends more on uniform repair than they do on our budget. We deserve our own section. It's the same story just about everywhere. No support. No recognition."

"And?"

"Well, I thought if I cracked a really big case, you know, get some national exposure, we'd get more support and the budget we deserve. I've been looking for a long time, saving up vacation time and sick time—"

Scott was losing his patience. He stuck the gun back in Ken's ear. "Is there a point?"

"Don't shoot me, please don't shoot me."

Scott pulled the gun back. "And?"

"You ever been on the Apollo system?"

"A few times, planning the dream vacation with the first-class seating assignment that I'll never go on, and the one you'll never go on if you don't stop stalling."

"See, that's what I thought. After I met you that first time, I said to myself, this guy just isn't the hacker type. I mean you don't have any idea what the Cuckoo's Egg is or who wrote it.

You're not a hacker, you couldn't have been the one accessing Apollo as a super user: QED."

"And the English translation is?"

"Someone logged onto Apollo illegally as a super user and input dozens of airline reservation transactions. I traced the calls to your computer in Baltimore. At least, I thought that was the termination point. Maybe I was wrong, but I'm not usually wrong about that type of thing."

"You're telling me someone committed fraud using my computer?"

Ken nodded his head. "That's what I'm telling you. Even better, they left footprints all over the place directing me back to you, almost as if they were inviting me to find the tampering."

"How did you find me in Miami?"

"It was the only reservation from Baltimore. I figured the others were bogus transactions and you were just joy riding in the ether."

Scott holstered the gun. "And what am I supposed to do with you now?"

"I figured if I watched you long enough, you'd lead me to your accomplices."

"So I'm still a suspect?"

"Not you, but someone you know."

"I work for the federal government—"

"Are you FBI? It was a local case when I started, honest. I would've told someone eventually—"

"Ken, I could give you a number to call and they would verify anything you need to know, but I don't think I need to do that, do I?"

Ken's eyes lit up. "Are you working on a case? I could help, you know. If there's a computerized record, I can get into it."

"Ken, go back to Miami Beach, go back to Hawaii, go somewhere. Stop chasing things you're not going to find. You understand?"

Ken said he did. Just to make sure, Scott walked Ken to his car. When Ken drove away, Scott followed. He made sure Ken was headed to Miami before he drove back to the Orange Tree Restaurant. He watched the place from a bench near a phone booth across the street until the restaurant closed around nine, and passed some of that time calling the Johnsons and Wellmen that lived within sixty miles of Summer Haven. Both endeavors turned out to be a waste of time, and Friday morning found Scott parked in a vacant lot where he had a clear view of the gates of Meadow Park.

Helen was still in town. Scott could feel it. Scott had traced Helen's every step since Miami Beach and this felt like the end of the line. Maybe she had found Jessica, but somehow he didn't think so. Jessica was dead, and his certainty about this was unsettling even to him.

Something here made the sisters feel safe. All he had to do was find out what that something was and in the meantime before revelation came, he would stake out the cemetery and the Orange Tree. Especially since the chances were very good that Helen would return to one or the other sometime soon. He had staked out weird places before, but a cemetery was definitely near the top of the list.

He was half asleep behind the wheel when the groundskeeper's son opened the gates of Meadow Park. He scratched absently at his right temple and watched the sun rise into the sky. He returned to the Orange Tree for lunch and showed the picture of Helen and Jessica to everyone in the restaurant. No one offered to help. He watched the restaurant from across the street until three and was about to drive back to the cemetery when he thought of Cynthia, and eventually, Glen. Glen wasn't entirely pleased to hear his voice.

"Scott, where have you been? Do you know how long—forget that, I don't want to know, just tell me where you are now. Where are you?"

Scott moved the phone away from his ear. "Summer Haven."

"Summer Haven? You found something, tell me you found it."

Scott rubbed his right temple as a muscle beside his eye started pulsating. "How's Cynthia?"

"Did you find something or not? We don't have a whole hell of a lot of time left. Ten days, ten days is all we have. Wellmen will be in Maui on the 24th."

"What are the doctors saying?"

"Your leads came through, you know. XWEH is Kexian Wong Enterprises of Hawaii, an import-export company based in Honolulu. Jessica had tickets from Miami through Atlanta, Houston, Denver, Las Vegas and LAX to Honolulu. A change in planes, airlines and names with every stop. Pretty amazing we were able to track it down but we did have the departure time and were pretty sure about the destination."

Scott shook his head, switched the phone to his right ear. "Back up, you lost me."

"Tell me straight up if you have anything because if you don't

I want you in Honolulu, yesterday." When Scott didn't say anything, Glen continued. "I'll take the silence as a no. I know you lost track of Helen, and I have every reason to believe Jessica made the trip to Honolulu. We have baggage checks, seating confirmations, all the way through to Honolulu on the 4th of December."

"The 4th? What aren't you telling me?"

"I'll make the reservations for you."

"First tell me what you aren't telling me, and I'll make my own reservations, thank you very much."

"What makes you so certain I'm not telling you something?"

"Because it's the truth, isn't it?"

"Her luggage was never claimed in Honolulu, and it's still at the airport."

"That's what I thought. I don't think she ever left Miami."

"Scott, call me when you get to Honolulu. I'll fax you authorization to pick up the luggage."

"What else?"

"What else, what?"

"What else aren't you telling me?"

"Nothing you don't already know. Jessica left on the 4th and was scheduled to return on the 10th, but you already knew that. Call me when you get to Honolulu."

The phone went dead. Scott rushed back to the car and took the Rand McNally map of Florida out of the glove box. It didn't take him long to decide on Jacksonville International. Jacksonville was only an hour away, at most, an hour and a half to the airport.

He was almost to Jacksonville when something Glen said clicked. Glen had told him he knew Jessica's departure time from

Miami, but if she had left on the 4th and planned to return on the 10th, what he had given Glen was the departure time from Honolulu. There was a rest area ahead. He stopped.

He found a phone, dialed Glen's home number. It rang three times before someone picked it up. He shouted into the mouthpiece, "What aren't you telling me, you son of a bitch?"

It was a woman's voice and not Glen's that replied. She was crying. "Scott?"

"Who is this?"

"I don't have time to talk, Glen's upstairs. Scott, come back to Baltimore."

"Is this Janet? What's wrong?"

"Scott, just come."

"Is it Cynthia, has something happened?"

"He's been lying to you. She's not getting better. They called Father Joseph…" Her sobs grew so loud he couldn't make out what she was saying. "… I got to go."

"Don't hang up, don't hang up, don't hang up! Janet? Janet?"

Janet's voice was so weak that Scott could barely hear what she said, and then even as he strained to hear, he wished to God Almighty that he hadn't heard anything. He dropped the phone, got into the car and as soon as the car was pointed toward the highway, he stamped on the accelerator and never slowed down and Janet's voice never stopped echoing in his ears. Hours later, aboard the flight to Baltimore, her words still echoed over and over and over.

Chapter 13

Baltimore, Maryland
Sunday, 16 January

Glen grinned into the mirror beside the bed. He hung up the phone a few seconds after Janet hung up. He felt the hand of God on his shoulder. Loyalty, you could buy it, you could win it, you could earn it, but could you rebuild it when the faith was gone?

There was a pair of black pants in the closet that seemed a better match for the jacket he planned to wear. He removed and discarded the brown khakis he was wearing and put on the pair of pants from the closet. Beside the empty hanger was a two-foot leather cord which he folded into the left front pocket of the pants, then started down the stairs. He called out to Janet, "These pants all right, dear?"

She emerged from the den. He watched her hide her anxiety with a smile. "Yes, those definitely are better."

He nodded to the jacket hanging on the coat rack in the foyer. He followed her as she walked to the front door. She helped him put on the jacket and brushed off the lint with her hands. She had the hands of an angel, her touch soft, hands smooth and cool as silk. She pressed up against him and kissed his cheek. He ran his right hand along her cheekbone, while his left hand caressed the leather cord.

There was an oak bench next to the front door. Glen sat on it and started to put on his shoes. "The keys are in the kitchen, will you get them?"

Janet walked into the kitchen. "Do you want something to drink before we go? I could use one for the road, how about you?"

He tied his shoes quickly, and quietly made his way to the kitchen. She had the refrigerator door open and was rummaging around—probably looking for the wine he had finished off yesterday. He came up behind her, grabbed her around the waist with both hands, then swept her arms out spread eagle, pushing her body up against the refrigerator shelves and thrusting his own body tight against hers.

Janet moaned and twisted her head in an attempt to look at him. "I'm not in the mood."

Glen thrust her head against the top shelf with one hand and with the other, lifted up her skirt. "I am."

"But Cynthia—"

"What do doctors know anyway?" He unzipped his pants with one hand, reached for the cord with the other.

"I want to be there, someone has to be there for her." Janet started crying and sank to her knees.

Glen rubbed his fingers across the soft leather in his sweated hand. He eased the cord out slowly, wrapped one end around his left hand tight enough so he could feel the blood flow to his fingers ebb, then did the same to his right hand. He stretched the cord out taunt, heard the wonderful snap mix in with Janet's sobs.

He kneeled down behind her, looking down at her as he did so and knowing in an instant he shouldn't have. He didn't want it to end this way. He wanted it to end the way it began. Why couldn't it end the way it began? Why did she have to mess things up? Why did she have to break into tears now?

He closed his eyes, inhaled, and all the while, Janet's sobs lashed at him. When he couldn't take it anymore, he stood stiffly, stuffed the cord into his pocket and helped her to her feet. "I'll drive. There's a bottle of muscatel in the cabinet, I know you love muscatel. Get the bottle, I'll get the corkscrew."

***

The taxi pulled up in front of the gate. Scott glared into the security camera. The gates swung inward. The taxi started in and right then he was never so glad to see the oval driveway in his life. He had already taken fifty dollars out of his wallet and was mashing it in his hand. When he saw the steps, he didn't wait for the cab to stop, he opened the door, jumped out and yelled to the driver, "Dump the luggage in the drive."

He beat on the door until Edward opened it. Edward's usual long, somber face looked even more somber. Edward said, "Sir, you're home. Thank God."

"Where is C?"

"The sitting room—"

He swept past Edward, ran through the house. The door to the sitting room was closed. Scott thrust it open, didn't slow down, and nearly knocked over Mr. Simons as he stumbled into a room filled corner to corner with hospital equipment. Dr. Haskins and Father Joseph were standing near the bed. He pushed past them to the bedside.

He didn't see the wires or the machines keeping Cynthia alive. He saw only Cynthia, the beautiful woman he had married. He grabbed her hand and wept into the layers of bandages covering her head. For a moment, he felt a hand on his shoulder, then later, someone pushed him into a chair. He sat, but didn't let go of Cynthia's hand.

Vaguely he heard the door open and close a few times. He heard voices as if through a dream—Glen's, Janet's, Mr. Simons', Father Joseph's, Dr. Haskins', Edward's. All the voices mixed into a rush of noise that made his head pound, then everything became quiet and only Mr. Simons was standing beside him. Scott looked up at him. "How long?"

Mr. Simons put his hand on Scott's shoulder. "It's only the machines, my baby is gone. I asked Dr. Haskins to shut them off. We were about to do that when you arrived."

Scott started shaking, a tremor that went from his feet to his clenched hands. "You what? What are you telling me? What gives you the right? What gives you the right?"

Scott reached out to grab Mr. Simons' jacket by the lapels.

Mr. Simons took a step backward. "I'm her father. You can't

know how terribly hard this is."

"How terribly hard?" Scott kicked at the chair beside him, sending it crashing into the wall. "I'm her husband, get out of my house! You plan to turn off these machines, you'll have to kill me first . . ."

Mr. Simons tried to put a hand on Scott's shoulder. Scott backed away. Mr. Simons repeated, "It's only the machines, my baby is gone."

Dr. Haskins and Father Joseph started into the room. Scott glared at them through wild eyes and clenched teeth. They backed out. Scott looked Mr. Simons in the eye, unclenched his teeth, took a deep breath and forced the tremor to stop. "I want the nursing staff back from wherever you sent them. I want to see all of Dr. Haskins' charts right after you fire the bastard. Now!"

"Scott, it won't help anything, you can't imagine—"

"Oh, can't I? If it won't help anything, then it won't hurt anything either, will it?"

"Scott—"

"Screw you!" Scott pushed past Mr. Simons and walked into the hallway. He looked directly at Dr. Haskins. "Call the nursing staff, tell them to return, then get out of my house! Don't ever come back, do we understand each other?"

Dr. Haskins turned to Mr. Simons. Mr. Simons nodded. As the doctor made a phone call, Scott walked over to the bewildered Father Joseph. "You were always Cynthia's favorite priest. Say a prayer for her."

Father Joseph loosened the grip on his bible. "I will, and for you as well."

Scott gestured with his hands, pointing down the hall. "I'd

leave now if I were you, follow Dr. Haskins. Edward will show you both out. Mr. Simons, why don't you go with them?" It was more of an order than a request. "You'll be the first to know if Cynthia's condition changes, so you don't need to come back or call. Clear on that?"

Edward, who was now standing behind Scott, grinned. "I should think so, sir." Edward turned to Mr. Simons and the others. "Shall I show you gentlemen out? Mr. Simons, surely you know the way."

As he walked away, Mr. Simons muttered, "Don't forget who pays your salary, Edward."

Edward replied, "Never, sir."

Scott nodded absently and walked back to the sitting room. Everything that happened afterward was a blur. He forgot about Helen, Jessica and everything else that had happened. The hours slipped away, the growing stubble on his cheeks the only thing that told him days were slipping away.

The nurse returned. He didn't look up, but knew who it was because for the past three nights she said, "Good evening, Mr. Evers, I brought you some soup. Made it myself, chicken noodle. I reckon it's still right hot."

He nodded absently and held Cynthia's hand a little tighter.

"If you don't start eating, we're going to put you in a bed next to her."

He beaded his eyes. "Maybe that's where I want to be."

The nurse put a hand to her mouth, set the soup on the table beside him, then rushed out of the room. The smell of chicken soup wafted to his nose but he wasn't going to let go of Cynthia's hand, not just yet. He rose and kissed her cheek. With his free hand, he brushed back a little tuft of hair from her eyes.

"I love you," he whispered in her ear, "I love you."

He heard someone walk up behind him, didn't respond to the purposefully spoken "Hello." Instead he nodded to the soup and said, "Take it with you and get out of here!"

"You're wasting precious time sitting here when the bastards who did this to her are still walking the streets."

"I don't give a damn about John Ellis Wellmen, I only want my life back!"

Glen grabbed Scott about the shoulders. "Keep your voice down. Your anger is self-defeating. He's got you eating out of his hand. God, if only you could see that. You want your life back, take it back."

"Don't tell me you've been sitting on your thumb for the past three—"

"My little excursion to Honolulu was a bust. I don't have your instincts. I brought back the suitcases, I want you to look them over with me."

Scott nodded to Cynthia. "I've got my hands full at the moment."

"Janet's in the hall, I'll ask her to come in and sit with Cynthia." Glen coaxed Scott to his feet. "It'll be all right. You need to think about something else for a while."

"Go screw yourself."

***

Scott sat by the bed and tried not to listen to Janet. Glen had left the room in a huff and sent Janet in a few minutes later. When Scott couldn't take her yapping anymore, he blew up at her and was now trying to make an apology. "I really do appreciate what you did, I really do—"

"I'm afraid of him, Scott," Janet admitted. "He's been acting like a caged animal the past few days. He stares at the walls. You know the leather-bound books that line the shelves in his library? He's been collecting them all his life, and now he's burning them in the fireplace. If you don't want to help him, at least go talk to him."

"You're drunk, Janet. You're not thinking clearly."

"I had a few glasses of wine to calm my nerves, that's all. Glen insisted."

"I'm sure he did."

"What's that supposed to mean?"

Scott saw he was agitating her again and became apologetic. "Nothing, nothing. I didn't mean anything by it. You said yourself the color is returning to her face. I'm not leaving now—" He broke off when the nurse came in.

The nurse said, "If you eat the soup, I'll bring something special tomorrow."

He tried to smile. "I'll eat the soup soon, I promise."

The nurse took the bowl from the nightstand. "Let me reheat it in the microwave, then you'll eat. Right?"

He nodded. "I will."

The nurse left. Janet said in a firm voice, "A few minutes won't hurt, a few minutes of your time is all he wants."

"Do you honestly believe I can trust him now after this?"

"He knows you too well, Scott, that is why he didn't tell you. I was there when Dr. Haskins talked with Mr. Simons, I was. I was there when he made the decision to call Father Joseph, too. We all believed it was for the best."

"But you told me the truth."

Janet said quietly, "Think about what I said, Scott."

He promised he would. Janet held his hand for a moment, then left. The night nurse returned with the soup. He watched her make her checks out of the corner of his eye.

The nurse said, "Mrs. Evers is getting stronger every day since you came home. If I didn't see it with my own eyes, I wouldn't believe it."

He smiled at her as she left the room, but didn't respond. He was sure she was just trying to get him to eat but he didn't feel like eating at the moment. He might eat later when the aroma of the soup overcame his willpower, but the truth was that the smell made him think of times past.

In his mind's eye, he saw Cynthia in the kitchen. Cynthia standing on the front porch waiting for him, always with a smile. The Friday nights they spent alone after he sent the staff away for the weekend. Saturday evening strolls in the moonlight. Sunday dinners on the patio. Cynthia lying in bed beside him, Cynthia who could reach into his mind and read his every thought.

"I love you," he whispered in her ear, "I love you."

His heart skipped when he saw her lips move as if in reply. He sat wide-eyed for a long moment, dumbfounded and elated. Her lips moved again. He leaned in close. She said a single word, "E-eat."

He smiled, frowned, then cried, couldn't help but cry, tears of joy, sheer joy. He started whooping and hollering. Janet and the nurse came running into the room, their faces painted with alarm.

"She talked," he shouted, "She talked! Get the doctor, call her father, tell the world!"

Chapter 14

Baltimore, Maryland
Wednesday, 19 January

Scott didn't feel right sifting through Jessica's underwear, but that was what he was doing, and Glen was standing right beside him, waiting for a response to a question he wasn't going to answer. "But how can you be certain the box hasn't slipped out of the country already? It's been three weeks. Three weeks for crumsakes."

"My sources tell me it's still in the states."

"How can you be sure?"

"They're very reliable sources."

"This isn't about fuzzy logic switching equipment, is it,

Glen?"

Glen said with a straight face, "Of course it is."

Scott threw Jessica's lace bra at Glen. "Then why am I going through the stitching on a damn lace bra?"

"At the heart of the box is a microchip, a very small microchip."

"What is programmed into this microchip? And don't tell me any bullshit, because I don't—" Scott broke off when Glen maintained the candid expression. "I'm going back down to Cynthia."

"A few more hours. If it's here, we have to find it, and if it's not, we have to start looking again."

"What's programmed on the chip?"

"Trust me on this, Scott, even if you never trust me again, trust me on this. You don't want to know."

"If it's so important, how can you be so sure it's not already in the wrong hands?"

Glen sank uneasily to the floor. It was the first time Scott had ever seen the weight of Glen's years upon him, but it was there now in his hunched shoulders, downtrodden eyes and sagging lids. He said two words, "Harry Johnson."

"And?"

"He and I came into the agency together. He was older, I was younger. We had similar backgrounds but toward the end in '85, we didn't see eye to eye on anything. He left the agency, went back to Florida. I stayed and picked up the pieces." Glen ground his fist into the floor and added softly, "That was the year—"

"So this is personal as well as—"

"You're damned right it's personal. I killed Harry Johnson

with my bare hands when I caught up with him a few years later. Jessica knew, Helen didn't, but either way it's personal. One of them has what we're looking for if for no other reason than spite itself."

Scott collapsed to his haunches. "Jessica's alive?"

"For the moment, I believe so."

"And Helen?"

"I lost track of her when you lost track of her and she was the only one who could have led us to Jessica. When—if we find her now, it'll be in a body bag. You can count on it. She was trying to sit on both sides of the fence—a dangerous game at best." Glen looked Scott in the eye. "Five days is all we have left. I want you on a plane to Honolulu."

"What happens in five days? I thought we had more time, until the last week of January."

"So did I."

"One more day, that's all I ask. I'll leave Thursday morning."

"One day."

"And the underwear?"

"If it was here, we would have found it by now. Analysis didn't find anything either."

"Analysis? Is there something you're not telling me?"

Glen picked up the suitcase and threw it across the room, then reached down, grabbed Scott by the front of his shirt and pulled him to his feet. He pointed to the wall. "There's your answer."

Scott pulled away. "What's that supposed to mean? Glen, I'm not a mind reader."

Glen leaned close and whispered in Scott's ear. "Janet's out.

That leaves you and me."

"What the hell are you talking about? What do you mean it's just you and me? This is bullshit, all bullshit. Go play your games with somebody else, I'm out."

"Loyalty, Scott. It's the most important thing. You can buy it, you can earn it, you can win it, but when the faith is gone it's all over. Without loyalty, you can't have trust, and without trust, you have nothing." Glen paused, sucked at the air. "The house of cards is crumbling around us. I trust you, Scott. You're the only one—and trust me, you don't want out. It's too late for that."

Scott started to say something. Glen cut him off.

"What you want is to get even, what you want is in the other room waiting for you when this is over, but only when this is over."

"Will it ever really be over?"

"It will, if you get the box before they do."

"And then what?"

"Always thinking seven moves ahead, aren't you?" Glen grinned awkwardly, showed Scott to the door. "Cynthia's waiting. I'll make your flight arrangements for Honolulu."

Glen held out his hand to Scott. "Are we good?"

"This is my house, I'll leave a room when I'm ready and I'll make my own reservations, thank you."

Glen kept his hand out. "You're making a mistake. I'm it, I'm all you got."

"Don't worry. I'll find your box, but we're going to do this my way from now on."

"Was it ever any other way?"

"When I get the box, we'll talk."

"I don't doubt that. Don't do anything rash, it's the only one."

Scott opened the door, turned back to Glen as he walked out. "Bullshit."

***

Scott gazed into her eyes. Beautiful, brown, Asian eyes around which his world revolved. He smiled, a dumb grin that wouldn't go away. "I have to leave," he said, "but I'll be back in a few days."

Cynthia smiled and blinked her eyes.

Scott moved away from the bed and poured a glass of water, offered it to Cynthia. His hands were shaking. "The doctor said if you keep getting stronger, we could get rid of these machines sometime next week, wouldn't that be wonderful?"

Cynthia nodded. Scott smiled. He heard someone behind him, turned around. "Edward?"

"Sorry to disturb you, sir, a telephone call."

"Take a message."

"Says it's urgent. I believe she's crying, sir."

"Is it Janet?"

"I don't believe—"

Scott's eyes widened. He kissed Cynthia on the cheek, then raced down the hall. The den phone was sitting beside the silent computer. He snatched up the phone. "Hello?"

He heard a woman sobbing, but she didn't say anything.

"Helen? Helen, where are you?" He switched the phone to his right ear, and pressed the receiver tight against his head. Behind the crying, he could hear cars racing up and down a busy street.

"Helen, where are you?"

She whispered, "Our room."

Scott squeezed his eyes together and tried to think. He heard the traffic racing up and down the street in the background. Our room. Our room. Our room. "The Ritz?"

"Is there life after death? Will I be free?"

Scott sucked at the air. "Helen, go back into the room and sit on the bed. I want to talk to you."

"The view's so much better from here."

Scott heard the phone slap against something and heard Helen wince. "What happened? What happened?"

"I fell, it's all right, I can climb back—"

"Helen, are you drunk? Listen to me, stay off the railing, go back into the room and sit on the bed. Remember the bed? Can you do that for me?"

Helen whispered, "They found her."

"Are you sitting on the bed?"

"If you were here, I would be."

He closed his eyes and listened for the noise of the traffic rising from the street nine floors below. "Imagine that I am, does it matter that I'm not? Pretend, you can do that, can't you?"

"I need to feel."

"I'll make you feel. Go to the bed. Close the balcony door behind you." He listened. The noise of the traffic faded. "Sit on the bed."

"I'm lying naked on the bed, make me feel."

"First tell me what happened."

"They butchered her."

"They? Jessica?" He took a deep breath, tried to think. Think.

Think. Think.

"The coroner's report said she was alive when he took the chainsaw to her. Will I be free then too?"

"Is the bottle on the nightstand?"

"Empty… I have another."

"Open it. Let's have a drink. I need a drink, how about you?"

Chapter 15

Miami, Florida
Friday, 21 January

Before Scott left Baltimore, he assembled the household staff, the nurses and Dr. Park, the new doctor he had hired. He reminded them that even if Mr. Simons paid their salaries, he did the hiring, firing and letter writing to any potential employers they went to after him. He also told them that he would be the one to tell Cynthia about the baby and no one else.

Scott told Glen he was flying to Honolulu and while he purchased tickets, checked baggage through and even checked in at the gate, he caught a flight departing for Miami instead. Things were getting too convoluted and he wasn't entirely sure that he could trust Glen anymore. How many layers of lies would he have to dig through to finally get to the truth? There were always lies, lies on top of lies—bureaucracy—but this was different. Glen had attached a personal agenda to a professional agenda.

It was a fast, pensive drive to the Ritz-Carlton in the predawn gloom. He didn't know what he would find when he got to Room 908, but he was hopeful that Helen would be alive—passed out drunk, but alive. He parked in front, tossed his keys to the valet and shrugged at the porter. He had one piece of luggage, his garment bag which he would hand carry. And it was during the elevator ride to the ninth floor that he had a sudden change of heart about not telling Glen where he was.

The elevator door opened on the ninth floor. He pushed L and rode back down to the lobby. He glanced at the clerks behind the front desk as he passed and to the group of gentlemen seated on the lobby's couches. Uneasiness in his gut told him something wasn't right, still he continued on his way to the pay phones.

As he was dialing, he heard someone walk up behind him. He broke the connection even before it started ringing, but kept the phone to his ear.

"Bad time for a conversation," said a voice as a hand reached for the phone.

He grabbed the hand, twisted as he spun around. He pulled the arm forward, smashing the guy's face into the wall. "Who the hell are you? Start talking."

He didn't wait for a response; he slammed the guy's head down, bringing his knee up at the same time. In front of him, he saw two others in the hallway now. A third man partially hidden from view behind them said, "Want to go for a ride?"

He looked at the deeply tanned face, the probing eyes filled with purpose, and the muzzle of a gun sticking out from a shirt draped over a well-tanned arm. "Do I have a choice—" He cut short. Someone behind him pulled the other man away.

He spun around, kicked, his foot catching the first man in the stomach. He went down, didn't move again. The other man jumped over his comrade and came at him full speed. He sidestepped, pushed the man as he went past, sending him flying into the others.

Only the first two went down. The other stepped back, waited as if summing him up. The gun, pointed straight at Scott.

Scott didn't hesitate, he continued forward, plowing into the speaker despite the gun. The man blocked and brushed Scott aside as if swiping a gnat. The three thugs were getting back to their feet, coming at Scott.

Scott went into a horse stance. His bent leg stance, helping him sway away from their blows as he punched rapidly: high, mid, low.

As they came at him all at the same time, he did a spinning kick, followed by a roundhouse kick, taking one of the men full in the head and sweeping him into another. One of the thugs came at him from behind. He ducked, bending at the waist as if bowing, his upper body going horizontal with the floor. He swept his foot out, catching the man's feet, sending him backward, but the man didn't fall.

He followed with a jumping back kick, catching the man full in the chest. The man went down, hitting the wall as he went, didn't move again. The two others came at him again. He side blocked a punch, low blocked a kick. As he turned, he caught a punch, grabbed the fist, the arm, then threw the attacker across his shoulder. A snap told him he broke the other's arm.

Screams confirmed this. A gun was fired; he turned and looked behind him. He lunged, kicking high, sending the gun flying. He missed a block as one of the other men came; the blow sent him to his knees. Thinking quickly, he threw a punch, twisted his wrist as his fist slammed into the other's chest. The man went down, didn't move.

There were screams coming from the lobby now. He heard shouting: a panicked woman's voice, a man's voice trying to sound calm. He heard clapping, shook his head because it seemed surreal. "Impressive," said the voice.

He turned; before he could get halfway around, the other was on him, holding him with two hands behind the neck. The man let one arm go, twisted the other arm back to the point where Scott felt only pain. That's when the man said, "Ease your weapon out nice and slow."

"And you're going to abduct me here in broad daylight?"

"Do you see anyone coming to your rescue?"

Scott's eyes darted around the hall. "What are your intentions?"

"We go for a ride. We talk."

Scott touched two fingers to the butt of his gun and forced calm onto his face as he prepared to use the gun. "And after?"

"The after is up to you."

Scott started to draw the gun; a well-tanned hand snatched it away. "What are you, superhuman?"

The man turned Scott to face him, putting a hand around his

throat, his thumb digging into the jugular vein. "Excuse my rudeness, I am Kim Dong Gi. Call me, Mr. Kim."

Scott sucked at the air, considered his options, wondered if he could break free, wondered if he would be fast enough in drawing the gun from his boot. He said through the pain, "This ride, where is it to?"

"Enough talk." Mr. Kim released Scott, slapped his hands together. Two guys in dark suits emerged from the stairwell. Two others came from the lobby. They herded Scott down the hall and out an emergency door. A black stretch limousine was waiting by the curb. The suits manhandled Scott into it. The limo driver slapped his foot against the accelerator and for a moment, gravity mashed Scott into the seat.

"Now we talk," Mr. Kim said. "If you talk good enough, we slow the limo down before we dump you on the street."

Even though the back seats of the limo were huge, Scott felt crowded. He nudged at the suits on either side of him to gain some elbow room—maneuvering room if things turned ugly. "I believe you have my attention."

One of the suits tried to backhand Scott. Mr. Kim waved the hand away. He showed Scott a video disc, put it into the player. He grinned, almost a smile. "Home movies are good, no?"

Scott's stomach muscles bunched in knots as he saw Helen on the monitor. "Don't hurt her…"

Mr. Kim started laughing.

The video continued playing. The picture wasn't that clear, there were a lot of shadows, but Helen's face was toward the camera. Scott watched as Helen began unbuttoning her dress, a hand reached out and touched hers. Helen smiled, slipped the dress off her shoulders and it fell to the floor. She wasn't wearing a bra, only panties. She pulled her partner against her and kissed him on the lips. He kissed her forehead. They struggled to the bed.

She lay down, pulling the man with her. She started unbuttoning his shirt, unzipped his pants, and all the while, blew in his ear. It was at the moment when the man started to rise up on the bed that Scott realized he was watching himself, and Helen.

"Stop the damned recording! Nothing happened, nothing!"

"I thought you like it, it is very good. What do you think poor, sick Mrs. Evers will think when she plays that?"

"You son of a bitch!" Scott jumped at Mr. Kim. The suits yanked him back into the seat.

Mr. Kim waved a hand at Scott. "I didn't make, I intercepted."

Scott looked at him, puzzled.

Mr. Kim took the disc out of the player and tossed it into Scott's lap. "You should concern yourself with why someone felt the need to have blackmail material on you and not with matters that don't concern you, especially if you plan to leave the business."

Scott examined the disc. "Are there copies?"

"Could be, maybe you should see who has the original. It might surprise you. Talk to Miss Johnson."

Mr. Kim raised his arm. The limo screeched to a halt. One of the suits opened the limo door; another pushed Scott into the street and tossed the disc, his gun and the garment bag after him. Mr. Kim yelled to Scott as the limo sped away, "I'll be in touch."

***

It was a two-mile walk on battered and bruised legs to the Ritz-Carlton. The desk clerk gave Scott a key without asking a single question. Perhaps he remembered Scott because Scott remembered him, perhaps it was Scott's disheveled appearance, perhaps he had been paid not to call the police earlier, but more than likely it was the pain-and-anger-filled glaze over Scott's eyes.

He got in the elevator, rode it to the ninth floor and limped to Room 908. He ran the card key through the reader and opened the door despite the "Do Not Disturb" sign.

The room reeked of alcohol and vomit. He noticed this only vaguely as he clutched the disc. He opened the closet, hung the garment bag on the clothes bar, then walked farther into the room.

He wasn't quite sure if he wanted Helen to be alive anymore, and almost positive that if he had known about the recording a few days ago he would have let her jump.

He went over the recording frame by frame in his mind. Helen had to have known about the camera because it was as if she had been posing for it, facing it, smiling for it.

He gnashed his teeth, and rubbed his eyes with the heel of his free hand. The stench in the room was not only nauseating but stinging. As stinging as the fact that Helen had been using him all along. She set him up. It didn't happen in the hotel, not like that. When it did happen, it was only because he had been drugged and it couldn't have been anything like the editing made it seem. He may have wanted Helen but he wouldn't have acted on those desires ordinarily. Still he wasn't an innocent in this; he knew that. If Cynthia ever found out and confronted him, he wouldn't deny it. He wouldn't claim to not know what he was doing. He'd admit it. He had done what he had done.

Helen was lying prone on the bed; a sheet was half draped around her naked form. Her head was hanging over the edge, and an arm was clutched around a vomit-lined trash can.

She moaned and he knew she was alive—with a hangover but alive, just as he had wished earlier but perhaps not now.

***

A cold shower, four cups of black coffee, eight aspirins, and still Helen hovered over the trash can. Scott had watched her for hours, but now ignored her as he set about examining the room. A camera had been hidden somewhere, but where? How much had it recorded? Who controlled it? Who would want to blackmail him and why?

He remembered the slightly off-kilter view of the bed and traced the wall opposite the bed past the thermostat which brought him to the closet, but he remembered looking in the closet and finding empty hangers. He heard Helen rise from the bed and go into the bathroom. He kept searching. If the closet doors had been ajar then like now, maybe the camera had been sitting on the top shelf?

The shelf was clean. The back wall of the closet, clean. He emerged from the closet and checked the walls adjacent to the bed. He found nothing, and his frustration level was peaked when Helen emerged from the bathroom. She moaned. Scott glanced at her and noticed she had cleaned herself up. He grabbed her, threw her onto the bed and tossed the disc at her.

He screamed, "Where was the camera?"

She looked at him, the disc, the wall behind him.

He bunched his eyebrows together, confusion playing out on his face. She glared at him almost as if she was looking through him. He said, "Where's the camera?"

She didn't say a word.

He turned around, sank to his knees to see from the angle she was seeing from. His mouth fell open: The thermostat. He scrambled to the wall and grabbed the cover off the thermostat, revealing a tiny black box where the heart of the thermostat should have been.

It was a tiny device, smaller than a pack of cigarettes, containing no tape, with a hair-thin trailing wire for transmitting on spread spectrum RF. It was the camera he would have used if he wanted to conduct secret surveillance. The kind of surveillance you could conduct from a safe distance and still see and hear everything.

He looked up at her. Her eyes were filled with terror. He looked back to the camera and saw the glow of a tiny red light on the rear of the device—the camera was transmitting. His heart skipped a beat, he sucked at the air. He put the camera under his boot and ground it into the carpet.

His heart pounding in his ears, he tried to think. He didn't know how much time he had, for all he knew whoever was watching and listening was doing it from the next room. He glared at her. "Why did you come back here if you knew the camera was here?"

She started crying. "If the camera was still here, I knew you'd come back. I knew."

He didn't ask her to explain. He told her to get her purse. He grabbed his bag from the closet and saw her suitcase. "What's in this?"

"Clothes—"

"Leave it."

He grabbed her hand. They raced into the hall and were almost to the end when the lights above the elevator doors stopped moving and the elevator bell rang.

He flung her at the door to the stairs, drew his gun and backed into the stairwell. With a hand clamped over her mouth, he waited and watched. The door had a narrow pane of wire-riddled safety glass and through this; he had a view of the hall in front of the elevator.

Two men clad in dark suits, racing out of the elevator and down the hall, were all he needed to see. He pointed to the stairs. Helen started down and he hurried after her.

Helen was out of breath when they reached the first floor and Scott was supporting her more than she was walking. He didn't tell her he was exhausted. He glanced to the lobby, to the emergency door at the end of the hall, to the stairs, to the elevators not that far away.

One of the elevators was coming down. Fourth floor. Third floor. Second floor.

He pushed her back into the stairwell and edged back with her. He closed the door to the stairs against its will.

There was a laundry cart in the shadows under the stairwell. He pulled it out enough for them to hide behind. He heard the elevator bell ring, saw a shadow move past the door and waited for a second shadow to pass. It didn't.

He hunkered down and waited. Her breathing was rapid and shallow. He clamped a hand over her mouth, heard the faint echo of footsteps from above.

The footsteps grew louder slowly.

He heard heavy breathing, wasn't sure if it was hers, wasn't sure if it was his own. He pressed his back against the wall, pulled Helen closer, and waited.

He was sucking at warm air that wouldn't quite fill his lungs when he saw a shadow framed in the doorway. The door opened. He ducked down, for a moment he was sure the suit had stared straight at him.

He heard footsteps directly above his head. A moment later both suits were standing directly in front of him. He knew this only by their voices.

One said to the other, "Did you see them?"

"Nothing."

"We lost them."

"I told you we didn't need the camera anymore. Audio would have done just fine—"

"We're not supposed to be listening to the audio in the first place, so how in the hell are we going to know what this guy is doing if we don't have video?"

"But we were listening—"

"Only because you repaired the transmitter. If we went to wires, you know the client would go nuts. I don't want to end up as gator bait, do you?"

"I told you this was mongo weird, told you from the start this wasn't about some guy's wife—"

"They gave us the slip, arguing isn't going to help anything."

"That camera cost nineteen grand. It's coming out of your share."

"It cost him nineteen grand, not us. You're getting on my nerves."

"We'll wait. He'll come back for the car, I know it."

"No, we lost him."

"Let's get drunk and watch the recording of those chicks getting it on again."

"And count on Harry the Wonder Clerk to tell us if they return? You're not only a pervert, you're stupid."

"Up yours! I'm going to order a bottle of cognac and charge it to the room."

"Sticking the client for two hundred bucks isn't going to help anything."

"Want to bet?"

Chapter 16

Miami, Florida
Friday, 21 January

Scott took Helen to the one place the suits wouldn't think to look: Back to Room 908. He paced in circles for a few minutes and shouted at the walls as he tried to think. How did Helen fit into all this? Maybe she had known about the camera all along but she was the victim here and not otherwise. The terror in her eyes, every time he saw it, was real, very real. There was one thing someone held over her, the only thing she felt she had left in the world: Jessica.

But what brought her back to the Ritz-Carlton? Why come back? What had she said about the camera—seeing it made her sure he would return. Had she really planned to kill herself?

Scott eyed Helen. She was sitting on the bed, hugging her knees and sucking her finger like a little girl.

Yes, she would have killed herself. There was no question about it.

Why would she have wanted him to come back here? Was there something here she wanted him to find? Surely the suits would have removed the camera if she had killed herself. What else was here?

It would have been a lot simpler if he could have asked her, but she wasn't exactly coherent at the moment. She was babbling to herself, nothing he could understand, and anytime he came near her, she started screaming.

What was here?

He saw her suitcase in the corner of the closet and dumped its contents onto the floor. And for a second time, he found himself sifting through underwear, only this time it was Helen's lingerie and not Jessica's. But it all looked the same, frilly lace, yards of red and black—slips, panties, bras, entire outfits. No dresses, why not any dresses?

"It's not mine," Helen said quietly.

Scott rose from his haunches. Helen was still clutching her knees, but she had stopped trembling.

She repeated, "It's not mine."

He looked up at her. She was wearing a thin cotton jacket over an oversized red sun dress. It was hard to tell what was under the layers of baggy clothes, but he had never seen her wearing a bra. "These are Jessica's?"

She moved her head back and forth slowly. "Nope, Pattie's

weekend specials."

He walked toward the bed.

She started screaming. "Stay where you are, don't touch me, never touch me. You promised you wouldn't hurt me, you promised you wouldn't let anyone hurt me."

He sat down on the bed, put his arms around her. "It was a promise I never should have made, but I can help you, if you help me. Will you help me, Helen?"

She nodded.

"The truth, Helen," he said firmly, "the whole truth. You knew the camera was there all along, didn't you?"

She nodded.

"Words, Helen. I want to hear it."

"He promised if I did everything he asked, he wouldn't hurt Jessica."

"He lied. How much of what you told me was a lie?"

She returned a candid stare. "Everything that counted was the truth. Everything. I didn't know where Jessica was. I didn't know where the gizmo was. Why did he have to kill her?"

"Why don't you tell me? How was Jessica involved in this, was she an agent like your father?"

"What do you know about my father?"

"Not much, a little about his agency employment, his death in 1989."

She started crying. "My father never talked about his work. He worked for the government, that's all I knew—that's all I wanted to know. But Jessica, she wanted to know everything. Her business wasn't enough, her degree wasn't enough, nothing was ever enough."

"Was she working for our government?"

"Our government, another government, what's the difference? It's all in her diary. She wasn't going to give it to them. She was just playing with whoever would play her game."

He grabbed her shoulders, and the instant he did, he knew he shouldn't have. "It wasn't a game. People get killed for the things they know. It's that simple. You know too much, you become a liability… They were using her, Helen. She was playing with her life and didn't know it, but that's the point. Make something look like nothing and get someone else to do the dirty work for you. The bottom line is to put the hook in someone else's mouth. They used her. Now I need you to tell me who they are."

"The calendar pages… The client was XWEH. May never wrote anything out." Helen's sobs intensified.

Scott sucked at the air. "All right, Helen. Let's start at the beginning. Tell me about the client. He brought the box to Jessica?"

"No, Jessica was on her way to meet a client when he intercepted her. He wasn't my sister's client and Jessica never saw him before that."

"Tell me his name. You have no reason to protect him anymore, and every reason to want to get even. Tell me his name."

"He told me his name was John. He gave me instructions on how to contact him and get him the things he asked for."

"A phone number, an address, what?"

"A P.O. box in D.C. and a phone number."

"What types of things did he ask for?"

"Little things at first. The names of Jessica's clients, what project she was working on, things like that. I told him to get rid of him, and if I told him the things he wanted to know, sometimes he wouldn't come and sometimes he wouldn't touch me. I wanted to make him go away. I wanted to make him go away forever just like he promised."

"What is WIH-2?"

"The project Jessica was supposed to be working on, but she said it didn't have anything to do with the Internet and that it was only supposed to look that way. She found something. She wrote about it in her diary, but didn't say what she found."

"You have her diary?"

"And her date book. The funny thing is, is that the book says the project came in as routine: Make a test port, test for FCC compliance, help the client work it through the system so the product can be shipped off."

He didn't say that routine for Jessica was probably never routine, instead he said, "Shipped where?"

She put her head against his chest and sobbed. "I'm so tired. I just want to close my eyes and never wake up. There's nothing left to wake up for—"

He hushed her and rocked her back and forth like her mother should have. He closed his eyes and thought about what she had said, and later, he thought about the conversation he had overheard in the stairwell. He figured the suits were staying in the hotel, and soon, at least one, and possibly both, would be dead drunk.

***

Scott waited by the service elevator. Helen stood a few steps behind him—she didn't want to be alone in the room and he didn't want to let her out of his sight. A few minutes ago, he placed a call to room service from a hotel phone just off the lobby, "We're back. Send another bottle of cognac to our room." Click.

A pimple-faced teenager was walking toward the elevator. He was carrying a bottle, whistling and acting like he didn't have a care in the world. Scott watched him and waited until he was a few feet away. "Just another Friday night, hey Ernie?"

Ernie almost dropped the bottle as he jumped. "The service elevator is for employees. You're supposed to use the main elevators."

"It's broke anyway."

Ernie pushed the elevator button. The doors opened. "No it ain't."

Scott said to Helen, "Well look at that."

Helen smiled at Ernie and walked into the elevator. Scott followed. Ernie hesitated then entered. He pushed 3. The doors closed.

"I remember you," Ernie said, "I always remember big tippers. You want something, don't you?"

"What room are you taking the bottle to?"

Ernie didn't say anything. The elevator stopped on the third floor. Ernie got out. Scott and Helen followed. Scott waved an Andrew Jackson in front of Ernie's eyes and repeated, "What room are you taking the bottle to?"

"Forget it," Ernie said coolly, "Some guy gave me a fifty just to let him deliver the bottle last time. The way I figure it, someone big is staying in the room, a movie star maybe, and I oughta get an autograph."

Scott glanced at Helen, put the twenty away. "Well then, we'll just follow you and let you do all the work."

Ernie stopped midstride. "Twenty is good."

Scott took out his wallet again. Ernie reached for the money. Scott said, "Not so fast. The room number first and the bottle."

Ernie gave Scott the bottle. "Room 336."

"Room 336?"

Ernie nodded. Scott waited for Ernie to get back in the elevator and for the elevator doors to close. Once Ernie was gone, Scott started walking. Room 336 was the last room on the right at the end of the hall, near the stairs.

Scott touched a finger to his lips when he reached the door and pointed down the adjacent hall. The door to the room was ajar, not enough to see into the room, but still not closed and locked. He didn't like the looks of it. He continued past the room, turned the corner, knowing that if Helen wasn't with him, he wouldn't have hesitated.

He gripped her shoulder to tell her to stop and took the .22 Beretta out of his boot. "Can you use this?" he whispered.

She grimaced. "The only thing my daddy ever taught me to do right."

"Can you shoot a man if you have to?"

"Don't carry unless you're willing to kill because the other guy will see it in your eyes and know you can't pull the trigger, that was one of my daddy's rules."

He looked her in the eye. "Would you have shot to kill when you found me in your sister's office?"

"No, not really."

"You shoot this, you shoot to take someone down. You shoot so they don't ever move again because if they get up, they're going to kill you. Do you understand?"

Helen gulped. "I don't want to, but I do."

He handed her the gun. "We're going to go back to the room now and do this just like we talked about."

"And if you don't come out?"

"Don't worry, I will."

She kissed his cheek. He glared at her.

"For good luck," she whispered.

Scott pushed her away, saying "I don't need luck," and moved her with his eyes to the place she was supposed to stand. He took the gun out of the shoulder holster, tucked it into the back of his pants, then knocked on the door. The door slipped open a bit more with every knock. He said, "Room service, someone here ordered a bottle of cognac."

No one responded.

Scott continued to knock and as he did so, he nudged the door with his elbow and peered into the shadowy gloom of the room. He repeated, "Room service."

Nervously, he waited. He glanced to Helen, warning her to stay where she was with his eyes. A little voice in the back of his mind told him something was wrong, very wrong.

He nudged the door again with his elbow and slipped into the room through the narrow opening. When no one shouted or screamed, he set the bottle down next to the door and took the gun out of concealment.

He was suddenly glad the room was shadowed in darkness and also suddenly very aware that his figure was outlined in the lighted doorway. He reached back with his foot and kicked the door closed, the soft thud of the closing door was loud enough that it should have brought someone running but it didn't.

It took a moment for his eyes to adjust to the darkness and a while longer for him to realize that the stillness meant no one was there. The room was laid out differently from his room upstairs. It looked larger for one thing, there were two beds for another, and the door interconnecting the next room was wide open.

There was a light on in the next room. He crossed to the doorway, then peered inside.

A lamp was on beside the single, king-sized bed. The balcony doors were wide open and the wind was ruffling the drapery. The bathroom door was closed, but he could see a finger of light under it.

He listened at the bathroom door for a long time, hearing only his heartbeats in his ears. Satisfied, he touched his hand to the knob and slowly turned it.

As he prepared to push the door open, in one swift move, he played his index finger nervously across the trigger. He thrust open the door, tensed as he sighted the gun from the sink to the tub and when he was looking down the barrel of the gun at a Jacuzzi tub and bloodstained walls, he closed his eyes and sucked at air that wouldn't fill his lungs.

He didn't look into the tub. He didn't need to. Two right arms dangling over the side of the tub said it all.

He raced back to the other room and brought Helen in from the hall. He closed the door behind her. "Did anyone see you standing there?"

"No one. What's wrong?"

"Nothing." He tucked the Browning into the back of his pants, took the Beretta from Helen and put it back into his boot. He raised his hands to his head, trying to think. "Don't touch anything. Just stay right there. You got that?"

"What's wrong?"

He turned on the overhead lights. Nothing in the room caught his eye. He raced into the other room and turned on the lights. A table and chairs pushed against the far wall next to the TV caught his eye; under the table was what he was looking for. He kneeled down, eyed the recording equipment and an empty rack for discs.

Helen said from behind him, "It's still playing."

He smacked the back of his head on the tabletop as he stood. He spun around and glared at Helen. She was standing in the doorway between the rooms.

He turned on the TV, saw static, ejected the disc from the recorder. The disc was labeled: 12-8. He stuck the disc back into the recorder, pressed Play. Helen came up behind him. He pushed her back with a gentle nudge and sat in one of the chairs.

The picture wasn't very clear and just like the recording he had seen in the limo, there were a lot of shadows. The room was empty and quiet. He saw an unmade bed, the nightstands beside the bed, and nothing else. He pushed Fast Forward.

Bright light from the balcony windows filtered into the room and lifted some of the gloom. Someone came into the room: A maid with a cleaning cart. She cleaned the room, made the bed. He didn't hear anything, turned up the sound, and still didn't hear anything.

A while later, he saw a hand, everything went black, and then when the picture returned, he heard a faint hiss. He pushed Fast Forward.

There was nothing for a long while, then something passed in front of the camera. He slowed the recording. He heard a woman's voice in the background. A door opened, closed. He heard the voice again.

"Is everything all right?" the voice asked, the volume so loud that it made Helen jump. He adjusted the volume, satisfied, he leaned back.

A second female voice replied, "Yeah, I'll be out in a moment. I'm going to slip into something more comfortable."

"You're not still worried, are you?"

There was a long pause. "Of course not."

"Well, I'm worried about you."

"Don't be." A door opened. "How do I look? I bought it for you." The woman who was speaking passed in front of the camera and sat down on the edge of the bed and for the first time, Scott saw her face. Out of the corner of his eye, he watched Helen bite the back of her hand. The woman was Jessica and the eyes, the eyes were as haunting as ever.

Scott asked Helen "Is that Pattie with Jessica?"

Helen rolled her eyes.

He grabbed her shoulders. "Is it or isn't it?"

"Sounds like her. Do we have to watch this?"

"Not much more, I just want you to be sure that the other woman is Pattie. I want you to get a good look at her—" He cut short as the other woman approached the bed. He saw the back of her head as she went around the side of the bed and kneeled on the floor next to Jessica who was sitting on the edge of the bed.

Jessica leaned back onto the mattress and her elbows. The other woman crawled up onto the bed, halfway up Jessica's thighs. She reached down to the floor for something Scott couldn't see.

Helen screamed, "Stop, stop, stop! Stop it now!"

Scott didn't, instead he held Helen in place so she couldn't turn away. He was rewarded with a partial view of the woman's face. A moment later she was dangling a pair of panties from her right hand and laughing, she rolled onto her back. Scott lurched forward, pushed Pause. His eyes went wide—wide round globes—and his heart skipped. Two faces were captured in the frame and at the same instant he said, "Janet?"

Helen said, "Pattie, it's Pattie. You happy now?"

He felt suddenly queasy. His toes tingled. His legs and jaw went numb as tension swept through him. He turned to her. "That's Pattie, you're sure?"

"Yeah."

He heard her confirmation, though he didn't want to. He sucked at the air, turned toward the balcony and the drapes being played upon by the wind. "Janet is Pattie, Pattie is Janet," he told himself.

Helen started to say something; he touched a finger to her lips. He heard something, a noise that didn't come from the TV because the video was still paused.

He reached for the gun tucked into the back of his pants, turned around. Just as the closet door directly behind Helen swept open, he jumped, grabbing her as he went down. As they tumbled to the carpet, he saw a flash, heard the muffled report of a gun, then another and another.

He rolled onto his stomach, aimed, fired. One shot. Two

shots. His gun didn't have a silencer so the report was loud and echoed in the enclosed space. The figure in the shadows went down, didn't move again.

He scrambled across the carpet on his hands and knees. The figure was masked so he couldn't see a face. He checked for a pulse, wasn't surprised not to find one.

After taking a deep breath and holding it, he peeled off the mask. There was a sudden emptiness in the bottom of his gut. He recognized the face. It was Edward. Edward, always the loyal servant, always willing to help out, always there when they needed him. Cynthia would be devastated if he ever told her, which he wouldn't.

A thousand thoughts raced through his mind, all demanding attention, all demanding answers. Janet was working for Glen. This was an absolute. But was Edward working for Cynthia's father, Glen, Wellmen, or someone else? And how did this connect to the recording Kim Dong Gi had confronted him with? Did it connect at all? If it was Glen, why would Glen need to blackmail him? He was already doing everything Glen wanted. What more did Glen want? Or was Wellmen trying to mislead him? In the back of his mind, Glen's voice whispered, "The bottom line is to put the hook in someone else's mouth."

He took a deep breath, forced calm into his mind. He turned to Helen. She was lying on the floor, motionless, apparently still in shock. Then his eyes found the spray of blood covering one side of her face and his heart leapt.

He touched two fingers to her jugular vein, looking for a pulse, as he asked, "Helen, are you with me?" He found a pulse. "Helen, are you with me?" he repeated.

He lifted her to a sitting position, found a nasty bump on the side of her head. "We don't have time for this," he muttered under his breath. He slapped her face.

She winced, opened her eyes. "Don't hit me," she whined. "My god, your shoulder?"

It was when she grabbed his arm that he realized he'd been shot, not her—the blood spray on her face was from his arm. He helped her to her feet. She didn't say a word. He grabbed her by the shoulders and held her there until she stopped trembling. "Grab a towel from the bathroom. Don't touch anything. Don't look in the tub. Wipe down the bathroom door handle, anything you touched, anything you think I touched. We don't have more than a minute. Go!"

He pushed her toward the bathroom, retrieved the disc from the video player, paused. He heard voices in the hall now. He staggered toward the door, switched on the security lock so that the door couldn't be opened from the outside even with a card key—and that's when the knock came, followed by a voice, "Hotel security. We have a report of shots being fired. Can you open the door, please?"

He backed away from the door, heard the hotel security person attempt to open the door with a security pass card. Thinking quickly, he grabbed the top sheet from the bed, wrapped it around his shoulders. He looked around the room nervously, nodded to Helen, who was still following his instructions.

His plan was to answer the door but blood running down his arm was soaking through the sheet and there was little he could do to hide the disarray in the room. He could drag the body into the bathroom but what if hotel security wanted to search the entire room? He could send Helen to the door but the side of her face was covered in blood. He nodded to the bathroom. "Your face," he whispered, "Wash, quickly."

"Your arm?" She mouthed to him, afraid to voice even a whisper.

"I'll live, go." He nodded again to the bathroom. He needed a diversion so they could get out of the room. The hotel had fire detectors and sprinklers, but he didn't have time or the means to start a fire.

The knocking came louder and more insistent on the door. He was sure Helen could get out safely through the other room if he could divert attention for a few moments but he didn't think he could get away as easily. He was wounded and bleeding. He didn't have a jacket or anything else to cover up his arm inconspicuously, and if he couldn't hide the bleeding he was sure to be spotted.

He looked to the blankets on the bed, glanced at the desk clock. It was pretty late; he could go out of the room wrapped in the blanket, pretend to have been awakened by the ruckus, race down the stairs after Helen. But what if someone had seen him come up to the room? Helen could slip out of the room alone but the two of them together would surely catch someone's attention.

There was no point in both of them being caught by the local police—there was no point in either of them being caught. He didn't have time for lockup, questions, and phone calls to D.C. He didn't want Helen to break down and start saying things she shouldn't—No, he had to get her out safely. It was the only way.

He did the only thing he could think of; he picked up the

sofa chair and heaved it through the glass doors. The chair went careening over the balcony. He grabbed Helen as she ran out of the bathroom screaming and pushed her toward the door to the next room. "Walk out the same door we came in. Wipe the handle inside, touch the outside with the towel. Do it quickly, casually. Move!"

"What if someone's in the hall?"

"Someone *is* in the hall," he said calmly, looking directly at her. "Keep your wits. Walk slowly and calmly out the door and down the stairs. Get the car, drive out of the parking garage and around the corner, like you're going to the freeway but stop just up the block."

"What about you?"

"I'm going to get your things and meet you."

She repeated, "What about you?"

He gripped her shoulders harder than he meant to. She winced. He ignored her, didn't release the grip. "We're going to meet at the car, drive to the airport and get on the next flight to Honolulu. You aren't going to cry. You aren't going to say a word. Do you understand?" He grabbed one of the towels in her hand, gave her a shove. "Go!"

She ran into the adjacent room, glanced back. For a few seconds, he could hear a tangle of voices from the hallway. He heard someone screaming, "What's going on? What's going on?" Then the door closed and he couldn't make out the voices clearly anymore.

They were trying to break down the door from the outside now. He heard a loud thump as a shoulder was levied into the door. The shouting and the frenzy in the hall grew louder. He knew he didn't have a lot of time.

He rewrapped the bed sheet around him, so that it covered his body and his head. The blood soaking through the sheet by his arm was only a temporary distraction as he stepped out onto the balcony. It was dark out, late, but this was Miami Beach, not Sleepy Hollow, so there were still a lot of people coming and going.

He looked down. Three floors below, people were gathering in the street. The braver ones were crowding around the sofa chair he had thrown out the window, staring directly up at him. "A jumper!" someone shouted as he stood on the rail of the balcony. Others shouted, "Look, up there!"

He waited only a moment, listening to the edges of the sheet being played upon by the wind, then he turned and ran back into the room. He picked up Edward's gun and mask, stuffing the gun into the back of Edward's pants and the mask into a pocket.

He unwrapped the sheet, letting it fall to the floor. He rolled the sheet around Edward's body, took a deep breath, then ran into Room 336. He dropped the body, reached back and locked the door connecting the rooms just as hotel security broke through the door of the other room.

Fortunately, Room 336 wasn't a suite. There wasn't a balcony outside the window, only air and a three-story drop to the pavement below. Holding the body about the neck and waist, he ran at an angle toward the window, stopped short, used the momentum to carry the body through the window.

On the street below, people were screaming and shouting as the body hit the pavement. Fire trucks, ambulances and police cars started pulling up in front of the hotel. Someone must have called 911 when they heard the gunshots. He ran for all he was worth out the door and into the hall.

The staircase was nearby. He pushed through the crowd in the hallway, didn't look back. Someone called out, "Hey! Hey, buddy! You!" He kept going.

When he reached the staircase, he went up instead of down, racing to the ninth floor. He wasn't sure if he was followed, wasn't about to slow down to find out.

Chapter 17

Miami, Florida
Saturday, 22 January

Scott pushed Helen into the window seat and took the seat beside her. He pulled her window shade down to deflect the glare of the rising sun and fastened his seat belt, good and tight, as if it would keep him safe—he loved flying and hated it at the same time. He set the morning edition of the *Miami Herald* on his lap, afraid to open it, afraid of what the headlines might read, and afraid of what the small red book folded into the middle of the paper might reveal.

Since leaving the Ritz-Carlton, he hadn't had time to think, but now he had nothing but time. His thoughts were moving in circles. He was battered, bruised, and the bullet that had grazed his arm was the least of his worries. Helen had dressed the wound; she was getting pretty good at using booze as an antiseptic.

She started to massage his neck. He chased her hand away, breathed in and out slowly as Flight 803 taxied away from the terminal. He decided right then that he'd call Glen as soon as he arrived in Honolulu. He would tell Glen the search was going well and everything was looking good, but he wouldn't say anything about his excursion to Miami, nothing about the meeting with Kim Dong Gi, nothing about Helen, Jessica or anyone else.

He leaned back against the headrest as the plane taxied to the runway, closed his eyes for a moment, only a moment he told himself, but when he opened his eyes they were already airborne and the plane had leveled off on its transit altitude. He thumped the newspaper with his thumbs, then unfolded it.

The headlines could wait. He glanced at Helen, who was sleeping, then turned his attention to the little red book and delved into the life of Jessica Johnson.

He found dipping into the private thoughts of someone strangely seductive, especially Jessica's thoughts. He had never kept a diary or a journal, though Cynthia did. He had peeked into it a few times out of curiosity, but this was entirely different. In his relationship with C there was a closeness, a oneness, so it hadn't felt like an invasion of privacy. But now he was reading the thoughts of someone he had never met, yet felt he had known forever.

Jessica's thoughts were as organized as her credit cards. He could have divided the entries and put each paragraph under subheadings:

Interesting/Ponderings
Likes/Dislikes
Work/Why I Don't Have a Life Right Now
People/Relationships

Today I watched a jasmine sunrise. The water, calm and cobalt, invited me for a swim... Jessica always started with Interesting/Ponderings, and always ended with People/Relationships. *I'm worried about Helen. It's nearly Christmas and she is still decidedly somber...*

Before Scott knew it, the pilot was beginning the descent for Dallas-Fort Worth International. In Dallas, they had to change to Flight 123. It departed at 11:20 Dallas time. He glanced at his watch; adjusting for the time zone difference that was an hour and forty-five minutes away. He continued reading.

The plane landed, finished taxiing to the arrival gate. He closed the diary, having just finished the entry for Friday, 29 October. Helen unbuckled her seat belt. He snapped the buckle back into place. "Stay put. We'll get off last."

✳✳✳

Scott paced in front of the ladies' room. "Fifteen minutes," he mumbled. *Where was Helen?*

At one end of the terminal was a cluster of departure gates and on this end, he could see souvenir shops, a snack bar and a newsstand. The newsstand was the closest. Its racks of magazines and books were hidden from view, but the newspapers were right there, right out front, demanding his attention. He glanced from the ladies' room door to the newsstand that was at most ten yards away.

As he paced, he thought less and less about Helen, and more and more about the *Dallas Morning News* and the *Fort Worth Star Telegram*. Which would he buy? Or would he buy both?

He started to walk to the newsstand. Someone emerged from the bathroom. He heard the door open and turned back. The circles under Helen's eyes were clearly visible despite the newly brushed on mascara and eye shadow. He knew she had been crying, just like he knew whenever Cynthia had been crying. You couldn't hide what was behind the eyes, you could never hide what was behind the eyes—the hurt always showed through.

Wordlessly, they walked to the snack bar. He bought a *Morning News* and a *Star Telegram* as he passed the newsstand. While she ate lunch, he consumed news stories, page after page, until all that was left to read was the funnies. But he didn't feel like reading the funnies. The lead story in the front page of both papers was the same:

FINANCIAL CRISIS GROWS, HYSTERIA DEEPENS

The accompanying articles showed that people were paying attention now. There was talk of a deepening panic, that people were losing faith in the financial and banking systems, the possibility of runs on banks the likes of which hadn't been seen since the Great Depression, but he knew it was a little late to start caring now; they should have cared before, not now. Now it was too late. Whoever was behind this already controlled the pulse of the markets. They could send the markets up or down on a whim, but there was nothing whimsical about what was happening. It was planned, carefully orchestrated. The rich and powerful were getting the message and it was a simple, clear message: We can topple governments, make and unmake billionaires. You can lose big.

He was back to the old questions. How do you attack democracy and win? How do you take control and keep it? How do you overcome immeasurable odds and survive? He knew with even deeper conviction that it wasn't by stockpiling nuclear weapons, dropping bombs or terror. It was through the fuel that drives our world, which contrary to general opinion wasn't oil, it was money. But it wasn't just about the money; it was about control: Control the flow of financial information, stop global commerce and exchange, achieve what others couldn't.

Answers were somewhere in his previous assignments. Glen had subtly indicated that this went back to his days with Harry Johnson and that he had recruited Scott into this from the beginning—whatever *this* was. Scott knew it was significant that he was the only one to come back from Munich, and even more significant that the Agency had singled him out as a traitor afterward. But if there was one thing he was, he was a survivor. Glen should have known this, but would Glen have bet everything on his return against the odds, or was it only happenstance?

He started thinking about what would've happened if he'd died with the rest of his team in Munich. He thought about what

Glen would have done without him, then he thought about what Glen had said, "You're making a mistake, Scott. I'm it, I'm all you got." But he'd known that was bullshit the moment Glen had said it. The truth was, he was all Glen had and Glen knew it.

He was just starting to connect the dots in his mind's eye when Helen poked him. "They're boarding."

He glanced at his watch, at the departure monitor just off the snack bar. "You doing okay?" he asked, putting his hand on hers. He didn't wait for a response. He got up from the table, said "Let's go."

They started back to the departure gate. He was midway through a yawn when he noticed she wasn't at his side. He stopped, looked back over his shoulder, didn't see her, but did see the ladies' room door closing. He shook his head and waited.

"What's wrong?" said a voice from behind him, "Did you lose your lady friend?"

He spun around, saw probing eyes filled with purpose. "If you so much as—"

"We are hardly barbarous, Mr. Evers. You cooperate and no harm will befall a beautiful woman. Do we understand each other?"

Scott beaded his eyes. "I understand that you're not man enough to take me down without an insurance policy, that's what I understand."

Kim Dong Gi snickered. "Do you want to go for another ride?"

"And if I said no?"

"Afraid I would have to insist."

"And Helen?"

"The rules are the same as last time. What happens after is up to you." Scott started to speak. Mr. Kim clapped his hands together. Two men in charcoal gray suits hurried to his side. "Our pilot is a very anxious man. I suggest we hurry."

***

Wellmen cut Mr. Kim off with a wave of his hand. "There are those who will never understand, there are those who will. Which are you, Mr. Evers?"

Scott laid the chopsticks across the top of his rice bowl. He was eating to be polite, not because he was hungry. His stomach was still bunched in knots, every swallow was forced, yet he made certain to maintain his composure to allay Mr. Wellmen's expressed displeasure. He looked up at the array of mammoth video screens mounted on the wall directly opposite him—monitors that currently showed a man sweeping a floor. "And you do this for pleasure?"

Mr. Kim snapped his fingers, signaling to the suits guarding the doors. Wellmen waved them back to their positions. "Put a man in a room, tell him to sweep it, make sure he believes no one is watching him, and see what he does. A shame that I can only relax like this on the weekends."

Scott chose not to respond. He had been on the ranch for two miserable hours, waiting in a dark room to be herded into the dining hall, and then made to feel about as tall as a gnat pissing on Wellmen's oriental rug. If he had a gun, he would end this right now.

Wellmen said, "I don't suppose you would be interested in a position as Head of Household?"

Scott looked uneasy.

Wellmen chuckled, then said to Mr. Kim, "Dismiss him, send in the next applicant." Mr. Kim stood stiffly and started to leave. Wellmen turned back to Scott. "At eighty-five thousand a year, they think they can be uppity, so I hand them a broom and tell them to sweep. Sometimes their reactions are quite comical—"

"Did you call me here to talk about your household staff?"

Mr. Kim lunged across the table and would've backhanded Scott if Wellmen hadn't suggested he shouldn't.

Mr. Kim doubled over at the waist, his back nearly parallel to the floor. "Forgive my rudeness."

Wellmen nodded approval. Mr. Kim rose, waited a moment, then continued out of the room. There was a period of awkward silence. Wellmen said, "He is overzealous at times but his intentions are true."

Scott pushed his rice bowl aside. The ornate clock on the opposite wall said it was 3:30 p.m. He was pretty sure he was on Wellmen's Colorado ranch. Denver time was an hour behind Dallas time; the flight to Honolulu had left long ago. He glared at Wellmen. "Exactly why am I here? Where is Helen?"

Wellmen smiled politely and dabbed a gold-embroidered silk napkin to the corners of his mouth. The napkin was identical to the one Scott held beneath the table, mashed in a clenched fist. Only the certainty that one of the four suits that guarded the double doors at either end of the dining hall would kill him before he reached Wellmen kept Scott in the oaken chair.

"You can tell a great deal about a man by watching him, Mr. Evers. You are a man who takes for granted a great many things. You insult me at my own table, pretend to be calm and focused, yet the flittering of your eyes tells me of a thousand ways of hatred. Once only royalty could eat white rice and yet you cast aside the base of life without thought."

"Are you American or Chinese? You make me sick, do you know that? You son of a bitch."

Wellmen seemed delighted at the release of Scott's temper. He smiled without the usual self-restraint. Scott lunged from the chair, knowing in an instant he shouldn't have, yet he found great pleasure in the fact that his hand came within inches of Wellmen's neck before the suits grabbed him and dragged him back to the oaken chair.

"A society that had gunpowder five hundred years before Europeans ever dreamed of it is not to be taken lightly, and without gunpowder, we would still be in the Dark Ages. Make no mistake, Mr. Evers, let there be no doubt, I am an American and my loyalties lie nowhere else. It should also be clear that I would not be the man I am today without the teachings of Eastern philosophy."

Wellmen turned back to his food. The meal continued quietly. Scott tried to speak several times, but Wellmen either raised a hand to tell him to stop or ignored him. When Wellmen finally cleaned his plate, he dabbed either side of his mouth and then turned back to Scott as attendants descended upon the table to clear it. "The only crime I have ever committed in my life, Mr. Evers, is the crime I carry out in my mind. I made a promise to my beloved wife as she was dying in my arms that I would exact revenge. While I believe in vengeance, Mr. Evers, I am not a vengeful man. I do not blame others for mistakes that I have made, I blame only myself. Do you understand?"

It took Scott a moment to digest the cold casualness of Wellmen's tone. He tossed the mangled silk napkin onto his plate as an attendant took it away. "Why am I here?"

"This is about vengeance, Mr. Evers, not for me, for Glen Hastings. He blames me for something that happened many years ago, something that nearly destroyed his career and his life, but something I had no part in. I am a legitimate businessman, Mr. Evers, and if I were otherwise, I would be in jail, billions or no billions. You must know that most of my wealth came from family money and all I did was invest heavily in ventures that turned a profit, I ask you, is that un-American? Or is that the American way?"

Scott bunched his eyebrows together. "If that's true, then why in hell am I here?"

"To end this harassment, here and now. I have many influential and persuasive friends in Washington; their reach extends all the way to the President. What's left of Glen Hastings' life is about to be flushed down the toilet, are you going to follow him?"

"Let me see if I have this right, you kidnap me and bring me here to warn me and—"

Wellmen cleared his throat. "We both know you came of your own free will. No one forced you onto my jet, you walked on. The reason you are here is that my daughter's wedding is only a few days away and I will not have her happiness spoiled by false accusations and harassment. I have one daughter, Mr. Evers, my only living child. I want her wedding to be a day she will remember for the rest of her life. Jessica is all I have left, I have spared no expense on the preparations, and no one is going to ruin it. Do we understand each other?"

Scott glared at Wellmen, suddenly seeing something he hadn't seen before. "Helen's not yours then?"

"Of course, she's not mine. She may have been illegitimate but I..." Wellmen's voice trailed off. "So you've made the connection, have you? You're a bolder man than I thought then, Mr. Evers." He stopped again, continued, "Do you know what it is like to lose children, Mr. Evers? Do you know how desperately it makes you want to preserve whatever you have left?"

Scott sucked at the air, looked away. He knew, a ball of white-hot rage in his gut every time he thought about C and the baby and knew that Wellmen was just outside his grasp. "Where's Helen?"

"Do you think I would hurt Helen? I've always treated her as fairly as I could. I've loved her in my own way. But I can't help that Jessica's my daughter and she's not."

"Where is she?"

"I would imagine she has continued on to wherever you were bound for. You are welcome to leave anytime you wish, but first let me reiterate that this is about vengeance, Mr. Evers. Glen Hastings is trying to punish me for something that I had no part in and no knowledge of until recently. Even if it takes a presidential order, this harassment of me and my family ends here and now. If you want to follow him into the gutter, that is your choice."

Scott stood. "And the financial crisis is what then—hocus pocus?"

"As you say, Mr. Evers." He cleared his throat. "My Leer leaves for Kapalua in a few hours. It would be most unfortunate for both of us if I saw you during my stay in the islands."

Scott walked away. When the guards didn't step aside at the door, he turned and glared at Wellmen. "Are the goons going to move?"

Wellmen stood, didn't say a word. Something on the overhead monitors caught his eye. He shouted, "Mr. Kim?" Seconds later Kim Dong Gi came rushing into the dining room. "That man, have security bring him here now."

Scott tried to say something, he was cut off.

"One last thing, Mr. Evers, if anything should happen to me or anyone in my family during my stay in Kapalua, I'll hold you personally responsible. I've made arrangements—an insurance policy if you will. I want Glen to live with his failure for the rest of his life, but you, I don't give a damn about. Are we clear as crystal on that?"

Scott turned his back on Wellmen and said, "If you're planning on killing me, you'd better do it now."

Wellmen clapped his hands, dismissing Scott into the custody of security just as the man on the monitor was dragged into the room. Scott didn't move. He glared at the man. Pictures, images, faces flooded through his mind: Was it John Tippton? Could it be John Tippton? He didn't have time to dwell on the thought. He was dragged out of the room much as the other man had been dragged into the room.

Chapter 18

Honolulu, Hawaii
Evening, Saturday, 22 January

It was 9:05 p.m., Honolulu time. Scott scratched at his eyes with the heels of his palms. The flights from Denver to LAX and LAX to Honolulu were the longest of his life. Wellmen was clever. Scott gave him credit for that. He knew enough about Scott to know that bribery wouldn't have worked. Still Scott found himself wondering if Wellmen was telling the truth and if he was telling the truth, what did it all mean?

Scott's thoughts were moving in circles—had been moving in circles—and the plane couldn't taxi to the terminal fast enough to please him. His thoughts turned to Helen. In Miami, he had purchased the tickets, paying in cash, in the name of Mr. and Mrs. Miller. Was Mrs. Miller, Helen, really in Honolulu as his inquiry revealed, or was she somewhere else?

He hoped she really was here and that she was waiting for him, but his gut was telling him otherwise. He rubbed his eyes again, and told himself that he would call Glen from an airport phone just like he planned. He would say the search was going well and nothing about anything else.

***

Glen answered the phone on the third ring. He grinned into the wall mirror beside the desk and waited for the Christmas tree to light. He wasn't surprised to find Scott's voice greeting him in a heated tone and the instant he picked up the phone a trace of the call began. Everything was going according to plan. He would show them all. Even monkeys sometimes fall out of the tree.

He let Scott talk for a while. He didn't listen. He didn't need to. When there was finally silence on the other end of the line, Glen said, in as clear and emotionless a voice as he could manage, "Helen is with you, give her the phone."

"I'm in Honolulu, Glen, I'm alone."

"Put her on the phone, Scott. I know she is with you. I know she can lead us to the box. She only needs to be persuaded that it's in her best interest to give it to us."

Glen reveled in the silence on the other end of the line. He could picture Scott's face in his mind's eye and would've paid well for a photograph capturing the moment.

Then a shallow female voice whispered, "Yes?"

"Is Scott listening to our conversation?"

A delightfully awkward discord of stifled breaths and whimpers followed. Finally Helen said, "No."

"Don't lie to me, Helen, or—"

"Or you'll what? He's not listening."

Glen was pleased with her sudden bravery, yet knew he could still reach across the phone line, always could. "There's an empty plot next to Harry's—"

"You can't touch me, I'm safe now."

"And Scott is your savior?" Glen chuckled. "He works for me, Helen, and I wasn't talking about you. I think it's about time Mrs. Johnson joined her husband, Harry, don't you think that would be good? Jessica on one side, mommy on the other, and no family plot left for poor illegitimate Helen."

"What do you want from me? I did everything you asked, everything."

"Though I would've taken great pleasure in it, Helen, I didn't kill Jessica. I was going to keep my promise. We made a deal. I promised to let her go when you gave me what I wanted, and I would have except someone else got to her first. I've no reason to lie. Do you have the item she sent to you?"

"She didn't send me anything."

"Don't lie to me, Helen; I know she sent something to you. Do you want to get even with the ones who killed Jessica?"

"She didn't send me anything."

"I tell you what, Helen, when I kill your mommy, I'll make sure there isn't much left, who knows, maybe they'll be able to squeeze what's left of the both of you into a single plot…" Glen's voice trailed off for moment, then returned full and steady, "Tell Scott where the item is, don't lie, just get it and give it to him."

***

Helen dropped the phone. She sank to her knees and buried her face in her hands. Scott grabbed the phone. "What did you say to her?"

"Only what you should have said to her."

"I know about the recording, Glen, I know everything."

"Everything is an awful lot, Scott, you don't know everything yet or you wouldn't be angry. Sometimes you have to cut down a few trees to save the forest. If you only knew—"

"Glen, I've had enough. You stepped way beyond the lines. I'm going to go over your head—"

The voice on the other end of the line became a whisper, "I know about the meeting with Wellmen. I know your every step since you left Baltimore."

"I'm going—"

"Don't play me for the fool. You're in this up to your ears and everything, and I mean everything, is sitting at your feet. Incidentally, you left behind a bottle of cognac in a hotel room at the Ritz-Carlton. Your fingerprints were all over it, seems to be the only clue in a triple homicide."

"What the hell are you doing to me? First the recording, and now this. What are you planning to do with the recording? Mail it to Cynthia if I don't do what you ask for the next sixty years?"

"You give me way too much credit, Scott, but now that you mention it..." Glen chuckled. "You see, it's this simple, you take out Mr. Kim, Jessica, and Wellmen. His estate falls into probate and third cousins try to carve his empire into tiny little pieces for the next fifty years. Neat, simple, direct. Don't you think?"

"If anything happens to Cynthia, I'll be coming straight for you, you sick son of a bitch!"

"I've never let anything happen to Cynthia. Haven't gotten it through your thick skull yet that Wellmen is the one who tried to kill her? He knows your reputation. He knows he can't buy you no matter how much money he throws at your feet—and the recordings were simply additional insurance. He's a cautious man, doubly so. Don't you understand how important it is that you're not on this case? An agent that can't be bought, Scott, you're one of a kind."

"Why didn't you tell me about Janet's involvement in this case?"

Glen was silent for a moment. "You still don't get it, do you? Years ago when we first met, I knew you were the one, the one who would help me set the record straight. Why do you think I oversaw your training? Why do you think I fed you assignments the last twenty years? Why do you think I positioned you where you are?"

"What about Janet? How is she connected to this? I want the truth."

"Forget Janet. Focus on what I'm telling you for a moment, will you: John Ellis Wellmen is the one you want. Bring him down, do whatever it takes."

"Damn it, Glen, tell me one thing that is the truth. Wellmen was listed from the beginning, and maybe Kim Dong Gi, but his daughter? Does this really have anything to do with a magic box or did you just make all that up?"

"We don't want you to find it. We never wanted you to find it. It's going exactly where we want it to go and it will do exactly what we want it to do. Helen got my message, she understands."

"I know the technology is valuable. I have Jessica's diary. She wrote about everything: The truth."

"The truth?" Glen started laughing. "The truth? You haven't been listening. Your truth is what I've fed you."

"I've recorded every conversation we've had on the phone since this began. I made copies. Who should I address them to?"

"You're bluffing."

"I'm recording this one using a device that fits over the mouth- and earpiece of the phone, transmits wirelessly to a recorder in my shirt pocket. Your system won't detect it; anyone you've had watching me wouldn't see it. Wonderfully brilliant, don't you think?"

"You're bluffing."

"If you're sure, hang up. If you're not, tell me about the magic box."

"Scott, you don't know what you're doing. Don't do this; it won't play out the way you think. You'll become a liability; everyone you could reach out to becomes a liability."

"Does that include you, you son of a bitch?"

"Yes, yes, yes. Are you happy now? ... It also includes Cynthia, Helen, Janet—anyone and everyone. Do you get it now?"

***

Glen slammed down the phone, threw the desk lamp across the room. Janet was lying beside the fire, half asleep, waiting for him. She jumped up, asking "What's wrong? What is it?" He told her nothing was wrong, but when he looked at her and felt the wonder of the hand on his shoulder, he knew what he would have to do, to her, to Scott, to anyone or anything that outlived its usefulness. Then he thought that maybe in the darkness as she screamed his name in the throes of passion would be the right time, but first there were things he must do.

He picked up the phone, pushed the second preset button. A strong male voice answered. Glen said, "This is Hastings… Yes, I know what time it is. Honolulu. First available flight… Yes, yes, yes."

Glen hung up the phone.

Janet patted the floor beside her. "Come here, you look tense."

"Maybe in a moment." Glen picked up the phone, pushed the first preset button. The phone dialed out the number to the private line for James Henry Simons. Unfortunately, the line was busy. He put the phone down, said to Janet, "A drive would be relaxing, don't you think?"

Janet squinted at her watch. "Do you know what—"

"You said yourself you wanted to see how Cynthia's doing."

Janet looked at her watch again, frowned. "Will he be there?"

"Perhaps, I'm not sure."

"It's like he looks right through me, does he do that to everyone?"

"I'm going to change this shirt. The keys are in the kitchen, will you get them?"

"Change the pants too," Janet shouted after him.

Glen continued up the stairs to the master bedroom. He called down to Janet, "What's wrong with these pants?"

Janet replied, but Glen heard only a mumble as he wrapped

one end of a leather cord around his hand. He felt the blood flow to his fingers slow, and as he walked at a leisurely pace down the stairs, his fingers began to tingle. It was time, he told himself. Better now than later, better him doing it than them.

***

Scott held the phone to his ear for the longest time, listening to the dial tone. He wasn't at the truth, but the layers of lies were getting less and less, and every layer he dug through meant he was one step closer to the truth. But there was only one way he'd ever get to the real truth, and that was to find the box and reveal it for himself, even if that meant confronting John Wellmen, even if that meant confronting Glen Hastings.

Helen's sobs brought him back from his reverie, and only Helen's sobs made him consider hanging up the phone. He did so and turned to her. She had heard every word of what he had said, and maybe some of what Glen had said. She was trembling out of control and no amount of hugging her knees was going to end it.

He started to grab her shoulders; he wanted to shake her like a rag doll; instead wrapped his arms around her. He hugged her because she needed to be reassured and because he needed to be hugged back. He hugged her because he had never felt so alone. He hugged her because she was next to him and within reach, and because she could reassure him there might be a tomorrow. He hugged her because he was positive Glen Hastings would be on the next flight to Honolulu. What that meant, he wasn't entirely sure, but Glen would be away from Cynthia.

The voices of the tourists gathered to gawk brought him back from the edge. Fleetingly, he thought about calling Glen back, but didn't. Then he tried to comfort Helen, but his touch only made her tremble more. Abruptly he stood and glared at the crowd gathering to watch Helen cry. He shouted, "When you've seen enough, get the hell out of here and leave us alone!"

He kneeled and grabbed Helen's shoulders. "What did Glen say to you?"

Helen said very quietly, "He killed her, even if he said he didn't."

"Jessica?"

"John, John killed her. He said he didn't, but I know he did."

"Slow down, how do you know Glen? Through Janet, I mean Pattie? You know Glen through Pattie, is that it?"

Helen's face flushed with distress. Her sobs intensified. Scott watched her try to think. She said, "John, John, that was John."

"How did you…" Scott's voice trailed off as the weight of the world hit him and pulled him to the floor. "That was John?"

She didn't need to answer. He knew it was true, perhaps had known, but before he couldn't let himself believe it. He put his back to the wall. The world rested on his shoulders. The whole of his body gradually went numb. Aim the gun, squeeze the trigger, kill someone before they killed you that was an inevitability, but the things Glen did to her weren't things any human being should ever do to another. He broke her down, used her, turned her into something she wasn't. Or was she?

He grabbed her hand and pulled her to her feet. They rushed out of the arrival terminal past the signs for the Wiki Wiki. Running, running. Running, running.

The Wiki Wiki driver flipped Scott off as he passed, shouting, "Hey, island time, haulie, better learn how to relax." Scott started shouting back, not because he was angry at the driver, but because he didn't know who else to vent his anger at. He didn't know anything anymore. He didn't know who he could trust, for all he knew, Helen was really working for Wellmen. Why not?

He wiped sweat from his brow with his free hand. The warm tropical air was full of humidity and the dark clouds overhead said it would rain as it been when the plane landed. They crossed the bridge connecting the arrival terminal to the main terminal and were under cover when it began to drizzle.

He pulled her past Burger King, past a myriad of shops, down an escalator to the H baggage-claim area. He screamed at her for leaving his garment bag on the plane and went to the lost and found desk to claim it, hoping it would be there and that no one had stolen it. He screamed at the attendant behind the desk, ordered him to find the bag, showed him the air marshal badge that was a lifesaver at airport security checkpoints. He screamed at Helen while he waited. And all because he couldn't scream at the one person he wanted to scream at.

Chapter 19

Honolulu, Hawaii
Sunday, 23 January

It was a few minutes past midnight when Scott stepped into Room 1208, set his bag down and tossed the keys to the black sedan onto an end table. The Outrigger Reef was a nice hotel. The room had two double beds and a scenic view—he had insisted on both.

Outside the window, palm fronds swayed under a darkened sky, couples strolled along the beach, holding hands and letting the warm water nip at their feet while gentle waves lapped at the shore. It was enough to make Scott yearn for something he couldn't have. Something he might never have, and for a moment his thoughts went to Cynthia.

Annoyed, he grabbed a fistful of drapes, yanked the drapes across the window, then turned to Helen. She was sitting on the edge of one of the beds, hugging her knees and swaying back and forth. He said, "Tell me again everything Glen, I mean John, said to you. Everything."

She looked up at him, her eyes the eyes of a child. "He said he didn't kill Jessica, but I know he did. I know he did."

"What else did he say?"

"Besides the bad things?"

"Forget the bad things, Helen. I made a promise to you. I promised to help you if you helped me. I won't let him or anyone else hurt you."

"He told me you worked for him, is that true?"

"That is the truth, Helen, I do work for him. I'm no saint, no white knight. I've done things in the name of freedom that make me wake up in cold sweats, my heart pounding, my head throbbing. I've done things that I try hard to forget, but my conscience won't let me." He kneeled next to her. "Did Jessica send you something?"

"You don't believe me?"

"I'm not sure what to believe anymore. So no, I don't believe you. I don't believe anyone… Think. A package, a letter, a postcard?" She frowned. He continued. "Her diary says that she found something, something that was worth a lot more than anyone knew. She told you it was worth a lot of money. She was planning on selling it to the highest bidder, was that John Ellis Wellmen?"

"What little I know came mostly from her diary, but I believe she went to Miami to sell it."

"You told me once that you had proof Jessica had it with her and that it was worth a lot of money. That wasn't in the diary. How do you know she had it with her? What's your proof?"

"I'm not proud of how I know, but I know." She paused then said quietly, "Right before Jessica went to Miami, John visited—"

Scott was silent for a moment, then he grabbed Helen's shoulders. "The date, what was the date?"

"The 27th, December 27. I'll never forget—"

"Are you sure?"

"Yes, I'm sure. He gave me a black eye and I had to call in sick for a few days. I was there Tuesday night when Jessica packed the suitcases. He insisted and—"

"Samsonite, slate gray hardcases?"

"Bought them last Christmas for Pattie, Pattie told her she didn't need them, and after one of her weekend visits, she left them behind. Jessica put those three suitcases into her trunk on Wednesday evening, put a brown leather attaché case on the seat beside her, and drove off. The gizmo was in the case because it wasn't in the office and Jessica never let it out of her sight. How did you know about the suitcases? They disappeared with Jessica, that's what I told Pattie."

He squinted and looked at her quizzically. "What do you mean by that?"

"I thought they were lost, that's what I told Pattie."

"Told Pattie when?"

"She came looking for them about a week after Jessica disappeared."

Scott jumped to his feet and towered over Helen. "When did

you see her and where was I?"

Helen edged away from him. "I didn't see her. She left a note in Jessica's apartment. She has her own key, you know."

"When was that?"

"The day after we came back from Tampa, after the phone call, after I ran away. The first place I went was Jessica's apartment. I wanted her to be home, I really wanted her to be home, but she wasn't. That's when I saw the note and after I read it, I called Pattie. I wanted to tell her what had happened. She and Jessica were very close, at least I thought they were."

He closed his eyes and sucked at the air. His thoughts spun away. The pieces weren't falling together as he had hoped, but they were coming together. Pattie is Janet, Janet is Pattie, he told himself. In his mind's eye he saw images of Janet and Jessica from the video labeled 12-8. Janet's presence at the hotel on that night was no coincidence. Her short black hair in the wig was no coincidence. Her presence at Jessica's apartment was no coincidence. Nothing was a coincidence. But everything pointed to the fact that Glen didn't have the box and didn't know where it was, despite his elaborate scheme. The question was, had Jessica known something was wrong? Had she figured out who Pattie really was in time to do something about it?

Helen started to say something. Scott cut her off with a wave of his hand. He paced in circles, tried to think. What if Jessica knew enough to be cautious? What if she had two cases: One Janet believed Jessica was taking to Whuthers and one Jessica tried to skip town with?

He put a hand to his mouth, turned and glared at Helen. "Jessica had a brown leather case on the seat next to her?"

"The beat-up case my father used to carry."

He swallowed hard, paced for a moment, then turned back to Helen. "The note, you said something about a note."

"Pattie left a note. That's why I called her."

He grinned. He had found that one piece of the puzzle to which all the pieces of a night sky attached. He asked, "What did the note say, what did it say exactly?"

***

By 8 a.m. Sunday, Scott had already been trapped in Keneke Kawena's tiny corner office in downtown Honolulu for nearly an hour with Helen pacing in nervous circles behind him. The office, a windowless eight by eight cell, was icy cold, nearly cold enough to see his breath when he exhaled. Ken talked the entire time, even as his fingers rattled the keyboard. "So you want I hitchhike the ether for you, find you your own cuckoo's egg?"

"My guns, you said you could get them back from airport security. Did you—"

"Email, no worries, a friend. But he knows you not a plainclothes air marshal, pretty obvious when you leave guns in a carry-on, trigger locks or no trigger locks."

"I had all the proper paperwork when I checked through."

"I'm sure you did, Mr. *Miller*." Ken paused, turned to Helen. "How is Mrs. *Miller* by the way?"

Scott sat down on the corner of the desk and slid a list of names to Ken. "Can you do it?"

"You're lucky I needed the overtime this week, otherwise Sunday's I'm out fishing or surfing with my boys and you wouldn't catch me here until Monday."

"Can you do it?" he repeated.

Ken grinned. "Strap on your seat belt and we'll surf our way in. Ever surfed across the highway before?"

Scott tried to be cheerful. "Sounds interesting." He didn't say that if Ken just moved away from the keyboard, he might have gotten the information he was looking for by himself already.

Ken's fingers tapped away at the keys. He glanced at Helen as she stooped down to eye a photograph pinned to a pegboard. "Good-looking woman," he said to Scott.

Scott looked at Helen. She was bent over further than necessary and that, together with the open neck of the loose-fitting dress, left little to the imagination. She winked at Scott when she saw his eyes on her.

Ken continued, "Not exactly on the up and up but I figure what the hell, I need the practice. That's how I catch them, you know, have to beat them at their own game. The latest craze, get this." Ken tossed a floppy disk at Scott. "Fuzzy mutants I call it. Got an advanced logic protocol from the realm of AI, but it's still your basic computer halting virus, only it's more of a plague than a virus…"

Scott didn't say anything; his eyes watched Ken's fingers tap away at the keyboard.

***

It was late in the afternoon when the Hawaiian Airlines flight from LAX docked at the arrival terminal. Scott watched from the shadows. He hoped all Ken's information was accurate, but didn't know why it wouldn't be. Ken had been too excited, too eager to help, and too thorough to have made a mistake. The only distraction was Helen, who had been flittering about the room, enjoying it when Ken's eyes were on her.

As Scott watched for passengers to begin deplaning, Ken's buzzwords circled his thoughts. When the doors to the gate opened, he put his back to the wall and buried his nose in the *Star Bulletin*. He watched a flood of tourists, ready for the sun, race eagerly into the terminal.

He chuckled to himself because he didn't share their enthusiasm and because he thought if he concentrated on them, he wouldn't see that it wasn't only tourists, there were wives and husbands and lovers and family, all being reunited with one another.

As the tide of disembarking passengers ebbed, Scott still didn't see Glen, but wasn't worried because he knew Glen well enough to know he'd probably take his time exiting the plane. Glen liked to make an entrance, especially if he thought there was an audience.

Momentarily Scott wondered how Helen fared in the new room at the Sheraton Moana. They had checked in early that morning as Mr. and Mrs. Patrick Greenburg of Kansas City, Missouri. Glen would get a laugh out of the suite's single king-sized bed, that is if he ever traced Scott and Helen to the room, which he wouldn't because Scott was still registered at the Outrigger Reef with their baggage and all their clothes still in the room, and the rented black sedan parked in the hotel's parking garage.

Scott saw stewardesses and other flight personnel passing through the gate. The muscle above his right eye started twitching and unconsciously he wadded up the Sunday edition of the *Star*

Bulletin.

He waited, growing more agitated by the second. When an attendant closed the doors to the gate, he gulped at the air, tossed the mangled newspaper in the trash and raced for the parking garage. Suddenly all he could think about was that Helen was alone in the hotel room and that there was a gaping hole in his oh-so-clever plan.

***

Scott leaned down, checked the Beretta in his boot, then wrapped his hand around the doorknob. He twisted the knob and slowly opened the door. The double beds were made up and unoccupied. The curtain was drawn. The bathroom door was open. The room, empty.

Instinct drew him to the closet. He removed the gun from the shoulder holster, took the safety off, slipped his finger across the trigger. An instant later, he took the Beretta out of his boot and did the same, then slowly slid open the closet door.

His heart skipped a beat as he saw a dark silhouette. He slapped the muzzle of the gun in his right hand against it and it slid away freely.

Out of the corner of his eye, he saw movement. He spun around, leveled the gun; a woman screamed. His heart beat wildly as he stared at the familiar face. The face wasn't Helen's, but it was familiar all the same. Still, he didn't lower the gun or remove his finger from the trigger.

He shouted, "Did Glen send you?"

Janet looked nervously at the guns, stepped farther into the room.

Scott closed the door behind her. "How did you find me?"

Janet offered a tense smile. "Followed you from the airport, you were driving like a madman."

"Why are you here?"

"Glen was going to kill me, Scott. I didn't know where to run, but I knew if I could find you, everything would be all right."

He directed her to a chair. He kept one gun aimed at her, the other toward the door. "Tell me about Jessica?"

"Jessica, I don't understand."

He spun the chair around to face the window, ripped back the drapes to let the sun pour into the room. He stood behind her, gripping the chair firmly. "I think you do. I think you know exactly what I'm talking about. Don't you, Janet? Or should I say Pattie?"

"Pattie?"

He spun the chair around so that she faced him. "Did you kill her?"

"Kill who?"

He stuck the Browning to Janet's temple. "Jessica, Jessica."

"God no, not Jessica. I fell in love with her, Scott, and him. I loved them both and still don't know why. Glen, Glen was different, dangerous, ambitious. He brought me into the Agency, and taught me everything I know. But being with Jessica, it was magic, like living in Oz. It wasn't supposed to happen like it did, but it happened."

He lifted his leg up, jammed his foot onto the edge of the chair as he stuffed the Beretta back into his boot. He kept the Browning pointed at Janet as he sat down on the edge of the bed across from her and stared out at the waves breaking on the beach. "Go on."

"You and I both know that if you want to stay alive in the game, you have to hold out. You see, I learned a few tricks from the old dog." Janet stood and led Scott to the window. The ocean was in front of them. Diamond Head was off to the left, the whole of Waikiki Beach below and to the right.

Janet said, "Scott, if we hurry, we might catch Helen before Glen does. If not—" Janet cut short as Scott stuck the muzzle of his gun against her bosom, then kicked the chair back so that it crashed against the wall and the window.

He said, "Tell me what you know about the box."

"I'm on your side, Scott; I'm the one who told you about Cynthia."

He glared at her. "Don't waste any more of my time."

"You're not like him, Scott, that's not you talking."

"There's two things in this world that I cared about, Janet. One of them has already been taken from me…" His voice trailed off.

Someone rattled the doorknob.

He watched Janet's eyes dart to the door as the knob turned and then the door started to open. "It's Glen, Janet, tell me where the box is. Tell me now, and I won't let him hurt you!"

Janet showed Scott a key, her fingers turning blue as she clutched it. Scott snatched the key from her hand, and leveled the gun at the door and waited, his thoughts swimming. When Helen appeared in the doorway, he nearly shouted for joy.

"You were right," Helen told him, grinning.

He didn't tell her that he hadn't been sure until a moment

ago or that the relief he felt at seeing her face was akin to being in heaven. Instead, he walked to her and flung his arms around her.

Janet began sobbing. "You can't leave me. You can't let him find me. I can still be of use to you."

He looked back over his shoulder. "I'm not going to leave you behind as long as you tell me the truth, you have my word." He turned back to Helen. "Anyone see you in the hallway?"

Helen shook her head.

"Close the door and lock it," he told her as he ran his fingers across the key. He crossed to the balcony, his eyes on the waves breaking on the beach. He needed some time to figure out his next few steps. Everything depended on his staying a step ahead of Glen.

***

The sun was setting when Scott, Helen and Janet arrived at Ken's office, the box in his hand unseen like the tin man's heart. Scott shook Ken's hand and said, "Thanks for agreeing to meet."

Ken suggested that Scott sit. He did. Ken rolled his eyes and grinned, like a boy waiting for a toy train set. He said to Scott, "Where is it?"

Scott set the cigar box–sized case onto the table. "Are you as good with hardware as you are with files?"

Ken's grin broadened. "Even better."

"Can you tell me what's so special about this that it's worth killing for?"

Ken turned the case over. "I'd kill for my cable box." He raised a hand to stop Scott from saying anything. "A bad joke, I'll see what I can do."

"How long will it take?"

"A few hours, if things go well. Relax, it'll be safe here. Last time I checked, this was a police department."

Scott grimaced. "All the same, I'm not letting this out of my sight."

"Suit yourself," Ken said as he turned the box over and removed the screws from the underside with an electric screwdriver. He set the top aside, then took out a set of tiny tools. "But it's going to be a long wait."

Chapter 20

Honolulu, Hawaii
Evening, Sunday, 23 January

Glen watched Scott drive the blue convertible into the parking garage, take a receipt and drive in, just as he had at the self-storage warehouse, only this time Glen followed more closely.

He drove into the parking garage; his eyes losing sight of the convertible as it went down the ramp to the second level. He parked on the first level temporarily, just to make sure this wasn't some kind of trick. The parking garage was next to the downtown police station, and he didn't want to make a scene if Scott decided to leave the garage without parking. He waited a few minutes, then drove down the ramp to the second level. When he spotted the convertible, he parked in an empty stall adjacent to it.

He stepped out, whistled softly and excitedly as he grabbed a toolkit from the rear of the truck, thrilling to the wonder of the hand on his shoulder. He glanced into the side mirrors of the tow truck as he passed, the white badge on his uniform catching his eye.

He kneeled beside the convertible, popped the cover on the toolbox and removed the Slim Jim. He supposed he could have cut his way through the soft top just as easily, but it'd be obvious that someone broke into the car if the top was slashed.

In fifteen seconds, he was inside the car, pulling the hood release. A moment later, he was looking under the hood for the ignition wires. As he set the bomb in place, he chuckled softly. It was enough C-4 to make sure there wasn't a lot left.

He closed the hood, wiped it clean of fingerprints and walked back to the tow truck. As he started the engine, he saw the fireball the bomb would make in his mind's eye and thought to himself it was a pity he wouldn't be around to see it. But the hand was guiding him to Maui and to Wellmen.

***

Helen and Janet were asleep, sitting straight up, side by side, on the small couch that sat in one end of the tiny office. Scott's eyes were on Ken, who was running a diagnostics of the box. The computer screen flooded with strange characters and as Scott watched page after page scroll by, Ken whooped happily.

Scott stopped gritting his teeth and moved behind Ken. "Well?"

Ken waved Scott back. "This isn't right."

"That's the third time you said that."

"And I meant it every time. This is embedded coding, in a list of some type, but I can't get at all of it. I'll convert it from hex to characters, give me a moment."

"It's a list of communications connections, you already said that," Scott said disappointedly, "and I already told you that you don't need to see it, you don't need to convert it."

Ken said quietly, "I knew that an hour ago. You see gibberish, I see words. I was talking about the code that is interlaced within the other code. But I can't follow it because I can't get to the base kernel."

Scott leaned over and squinted his eyes at the insides of the box. "Try a different chip."

"This is the one. Damned Flash ROM, maybe if I just dumped the code and then flashed it, maybe I'd be able to see what was hidden in the base."

Scott's eyes widened. "Dump?"

"Download, of course, except for the base I can't get to, but I know it's there, there's always a tiny bit of code that is unerasable on a Flash ROM. Some larger, some smaller, but always there."

Scott heard Helen's yawn and cocked his head in her direction. She was curled up, practically in Janet's lap now.

"I'm hungry," she said. "You guys hungry? Burgers sound good?"

Ken replied quickly. "Zippy's three blocks down. I'll have a large chili and a bacon burger."

Helen stretched out, her feet hanging over the edge of the couch. She sat up, reached for the car keys. Janet peeled open her eyelids. "Coffee," she whispered, "it's got to be better than the coffee here."

Helen jingled the keys in her hand and smiled at Scott. "There's a bacon burger with your name on it."

Scott glared at her. "No one goes anywhere alone; we all leave together." He took a handful of change out of his pocket and handed it to Helen. "I saw vending machines by the coffee maker."

Helen turned up her lip and was just about to leave the room when Ken grabbed Scott's arm. "I'm in!" he shouted, "Will you look at that, better than anything Rubik could have—" Ken cut himself off with a hiss and muttered in a voice Scott barely understood, "Dear God, there's a virus attached. It's going to wipe out the code."

Scott sank to his knees, the weight of the world rested on his shoulders. He whispered words from the voice clawing at the back of his mind, "The future is information. Those who control information, control the future."

Ken mumbled, "No, wait, it's… It's attacking my computer. I can't get this, I can't get this," as his fingers pounded away at the keys. He stopped typing for a moment, grabbed Scott's shoulder. "Get the disc case, there's an orange disc in there. Hurry."

Scott made a grab for the disc case on the other end of the desk. It was on the top shelf. Books went flying. He fumbled through the discs in the case looking for an orange one, found it, handed it to Ken who inserted it into the waiting disc drive.

Ken went back to typing fast and furious. Scott stumbled onto the couch in the place Helen had been occupying until a few minutes ago. He scratched at his right temple as he fought to think through everything Glen had told him about the box and Wellmen. And then he wondered why he was sitting here and where was Glen and why wasn't Glen in Honolulu?

Scott stood. "We've been here too long. I don't like the feel of this anymore. Disconnect, get out."

"I'm there, I'm almost there."

Scott grabbed Ken's hands. "No stop, you don't understand. You don't want to know the truth that's there; I can't let you continue. There's too much at risk here and if the people behind this even suspect that you know too much, you're a walking dead man. Put the case back together. Wipe all records of what we've been doing from your computer."

"You don't understand, the virus is already doing it. It's wiping out everything."

"Let it finish then, but disconnect everything. Put it all back together."

"But my computer, everything's there. All my work, my—"

"Let it finish. You have backups don't you?"

"Last month."

Scott patted Ken's shoulder. "Better to lose a month's work than your life. I think we found enough."

"We did?"

Scott smiled reassuringly. "Yes, we did. You were a great help, but now I have to ask you a big favor. I have to ask you to forget about the box, everything. Can you do that for me?"

Ken nodded, went to work putting the box back together.

Scott paced in nervous little circles. A few minutes passed, then he asked, "How easy would it be to go to Maui by boat?"

"As easy as taking a fishing charter in the morning. I'll make a call to a buddy of mine and get us a boat."

"*Us?* Go home to your wife and kids."

"You need me."

Scott shook his head.

"I know too much."

"I told you to forget what you know." Scott picked up his keys from the desk. "Make the phone call."

Scott chased Helen off to the vending machine while Ken dialed the phone. By the time she returned with munchies, Ken had the captain of the Sea Walker agreeing to a 5 a.m. charter. When he hung up the phone, Ken turned to Scott and said, "Let me take you to the boat in the morning. I didn't tell him you wanted to go all the way to Maui. He thinks you're a standard charter, someone I know from the San Francisco P.D."

"What if we wanted to leave sooner than 5 a.m.? Could you call him from the marina and convince him to meet us?"

"Now?"

"Now."

"You wouldn't want to do it at night, too much can go wrong out there."

"Would he agree to meet us?"

"Wouldn't have to meet us, lives on the boat. He's there now, that's not the problem. The problem is motoring to Maui now."

"Our problem, not yours." Scott tucked the case into his left sport coat pocket, grabbed a bag of chips and opened it as he walked into the corridor. He glanced back over his shoulder as he walked to the elevator to make sure the others followed, but his thoughts were elsewhere. He took the elevator up and then walked across the pedestrian walkway to the adjacent parking garage.

When the garage elevator stopped on Level Two and the doors opened, Scott was the first to exit. He ran his fingers across the ignition key as he walked to the car. Janet, Ken and Helen were a few steps behind him—at least he thought they were. He opened the car door, slipped the key into the ignition, was about to turn the car over, and only then realized he was alone. He had a clear view to the elevator and could see Janet but not the others. He thought about starting the car and driving over to her, but beeped the horn instead. He yelled, "Hurry up!"

He thumped the steering wheel while he waited impatiently, his right hand going to the key in the ignition as his patience came to an end. Just then Janet opened the passenger door. He told her, "Just like last time, get in the back seat, and stay out of sight."

"It's dark out," Janet complained.

"Where's Ken?"

"Waiting for Helen by the elevator, I think she went to the bathroom."

Scott's eyes went wide. "When?"

"I'm not sure."

Scott's heart skipped. He touched his thumb and forefinger to the key in the ignition. He wanted to start the car to get ready to go; he was anxious to get away but didn't know why. He paused, thinking, removed the keys. "Stay put, I'll be right back."

He jumped out of the car and raced to the elevator, tossing the keys to Ken as they met. "I'm going to find Helen, get in the driver's seat and wait for me. Something doesn't feel right."

Scott pushed the elevator's Up button, his eyes wandering to the sign for the stairs to his left. He was halfway to the stairs when the elevator's bell dinged. He spun around, raced back to the elevator and slammed into Helen as he ran inside. "Jesus, where were you?"

Helen smiled and said, "Bathroom." She waved to Ken in the car.

As Scott started to turn around, his eyes toward the car, he heard the engine turn over. There was a sickening feeling in the bottom of his gut as he realized something wasn't right and an instant later, an explosion knocked him to the cold cement of the parking garage. Helen was at his feet, he crawled over to her, wrapped his arms around her, his body over hers shielding her.

He cut off Helen's screams with a cupped hand and dragged her toward the stairwell. Just as the door to the stairwell clicked shut, a second explosion rocked the parking garage. The gas tank on an adjacent car burst and the car went up in flames.

Scott pulled Helen to her feet and propelled her toward the stairs. Two flights of stairs lay between them and the street. He passed Helen, taking the stairs two at a time, pulling her behind him.

As they reached the exit door, they heard sirens sounding from several different directions. Scott paused, poked his head out. Squad cars were pulling up in front of the garage. Officers were running toward the street entrance from the police station. Just then there was a third explosion.

Helen raced out into the street in front of him. There was another parking structure next door. She ran toward the street-level entry door. Scott followed.

***

Someone grabbed Scott's arm and twisted; it wasn't Helen. The grip was strong, viselike. The assailant shouted, "What do you know?" Scott broke away, moved into a defensive stance with Helen behind him. The assailant repeated, "What do you know?"

Scott turned, attempting to move back to the entry door. It was kicked closed in his face. He drew his Browning; it was kicked out of his hand.

"Not yet," the assailant shouted.

Scott launched forward, like a bull, knocking the other man off his feet. He grabbed the man around the neck, thrusting the man's head back into the concrete. He wrestled the other onto his stomach. As the man turned back to him, screaming, Scott's face showed recognition and confusion. "John? John Tippton?"

John's elbow shot back, catching Scott in the throat. "Surprised you remembered."

Scott reeled back. John turned over, his foot sweeping out, catching Scott's leg. Scott held firm, didn't go down. "Colorado, you were there. What in the world are you doing? Do you know what you're doing?"

John jumped to his feet. The two squared off. "I'm a survivor, Scott. If there's one thing you should know about me, it's that. You do what it takes, whatever the price." John circled, moving Scott into the corner of the stairwell, making sure he was between the door and Scott. "Didn't expect to see me after that, did you?"

Scott grabbed Helen and pulled her toward him. "What do you want?"

"You know what I want." John started laughing.

Helen screamed. Scott stamped on her foot and pushed her

back into the wall behind him. "You can't have it."

John cocked back the hammer on his gun. The clip had fourteen rounds. He suspected he'd need only two or three. "You've got it wrong, all wrong. I get her, he gets the package."

Scott turned and for the first time saw what Helen had seen just then. "Glen?"

Glen emerged from the shadows, glared at Helen. He was armed with a pump-action shotgun. "This wasn't part of the bargain. He wasn't supposed to be here. He was supposed to be in the car."

Scott expected the response to come from John, but it came from Helen. "I don't control his actions. How was I to know he'd come back for me? Damned fool. He has the box though, so it worked out just as well."

Helen moved out from behind Scott, reached into his shirt pocket and grabbed the box. Tears were streaming down her cheeks. She backed away from Scott, toward John. "You killed Janet, you son of a bitch. That wasn't part of the bargain!"

Scott looked to Glen, expecting the response to come from him but it didn't. Instead, it came from John. "Janet was a liability a long time ago. You knew that. You said you understood."

Scott raised his hands to his head and shouted, "What the hell is going on?"

Helen turned back to Scott, kicked him in the groin. As he went down, she kneed him in the face. "Poor little, Helen, poor little, Helen! Not good enough to love, but good enough to screw. Always good enough for everybody to screw. How's it feel, Scott?" She kicked him again. "That's for May."

Scott shouted, "I didn't have anything to do with May's death!"

Helen kicked him. "Liar, you weren't getting the message. That's why May had to die."

Scott backed away into the wall. Helen came at him, kicking and punching. "For Mark and Kevin!"

Scott defended himself but didn't fight back. "Who? You're insane!"

She shouted, "Newsflash, Helen's insane!"

Scott looked at Glen just as she came at him again. "Why?"

John stepped toward Helen, grabbed the back of her neck, shouted, "Enough." He turned Helen to him, then he turned to Glen, his gun still pointed at Scott, "I've delivered. Your turn."

Glen threw a duffle bag at John's feet. "Everything you asked for is there."

John glared. "I don't believe you." He leaned down, unzipped the bag and started rummaging through the contents, his gun pointed at Glen now. "No double cross this time?"

"That was an act, do you think we were entirely alone? Had to look real, dotted I's and crossed T's. And if I remember correctly, you're the one who took it too far. Hell of a jam you left me in …" Glen paused, looked to Scott, continued. "The handheld's in the bottom of the case. Touch the screen and it will come on. You'll have direct access to your records and accounts over wireless. It's all there."

John searched through the duffle bag with one hand, when he stood he was holding a small handheld PC. He handed the device to Helen.

"What, don't trust me? They're your accounts, why don't—"

Midstream Glen stopped, turned, lunged away just as the device exploded in Helen's face, the blast knocking her back into the door and taking John with her. Glen rolled, fired, pumped the shotgun, fired again. The second shot hit John in the chest, stunning him momentarily despite his protective vest. John started firing as fast as he could pull the trigger. Glen pumped the shotgun, fired. John didn't move afterward.

Glen rolled back, pointed the gun where Scott should have been, only to find Scott was gone. He shouted, "Scott, this isn't over. This isn't over!"

He stood, looked around, threw his hands up in the air. He started talking to himself, went over to the duffle bag and picked it up. He looked around for the box. When he couldn't find it, he grew angry, started shouting. Suddenly enraged, he kicked John to make sure he was dead, then leaned over to feel for a pulse.

He kicked Helen's body the same way he had kicked John's. The body twitched and moved. Glen leaned down next to Helen, checking for a pulse. He pumped the shotgun, turned to look behind him, making sure no one was around, then fired. The shotgun blast blew chunks out of the wall.

He leaned down, checked Helen's body again. Satisfied, he repositioned John's body, then placed the shotgun next to John. He wasn't worried about fingerprints, the gloves he wore took care of that. He removed his overcoat, stuffed it into the duffle bag, then slipped out the door, holding the bag.

Outside sirens were screaming and someone was on a loudspeaker asking people to move back as Honolulu P.D. cordoned off the entrance to the adjacent parking garage. Glen slipped into the crowd. As he walked, he looked around, half expecting Scott to be somewhere in the growing throng.

Casually, he walked over to the closest emergency vehicle. Took a badge out of his pocket and flashed it to a paramedic. "Were you the first on the scene?"

The paramedic shrugged. "Hell, I don't know. It's a mess."

"Did you see anyone run through those doors over there?" Glen pointed to the door he had just come out of.

The paramedic shrugged again. "Like I said, I don't know. It's crazy."

A nearby police officer came over, apparently hearing the conversation.

Glen showed the officer his badge, introduced himself as Jacob Henderson FBI and asked, "Were you the first on the scene, captain?"

"Sergeant, and no, not me." The officer pointed to a group of patrolmen. "They arrived first. They're briefing the captain. Hell of thing to happen next to the station. Looks like two fatalities."

"Two, you sure?"

The officer keyed the mobile handset that was clipped to his shirt. "2-5, I'm at the scene." A response came back over the radio. The officer turned his attention back to Glen. "Yeah, that's what they're saying over the radio."

Glen bobbed his head, said, "All right, thanks." He started to turn away, then turned back. "You didn't happen to see three individuals run into that parking garage?"

The officer shook his head. "No, I just got here. Do you want me to check it out?"

Glen put his arm around the officer's shoulder. "Why don't you do that. Take some back up with you just in case." He took a picture out of an inside pocket, handed it to the officer. "One of the men I'm looking for. He's wanted for a triple homicide in Florida. He's the one I suspect in the car bombing. Catch him, and you'll be well on your way to lieutenant. Do we understand each other, sergeant?"

All too eager to please, the officer hurried off. Glen nodded and turned away, satisfied.

Chapter 21

Kapalua, Hawaii
Thursday, 27 January

Glen sat as the waiter indicated. "Coffee, sir?" the waiter asked.

"No, no coffee," he said, "it gives me the jitters. A glass of fresh guava juice would be nice. Could you find me a morning newspaper?"

The waiter hurried off, returned a few minutes later with the juice and a paper.

Glen took a sip of guava juice, then unfolded the paper. His eyes homing in on the headlines:

Killer At Large, Victim Count Rises

He chuckled softly at the picture of Scott Madison Evers in

the middle of the article and took another sip of juice.

He took a pre-paid express mail envelope out of his pocket, unfolded it, and set it on the table top. He stuffed the paper and a box into it then took a pen out of his shirt pocket. He hastily wrote an address, and was sealing the envelope when the waiter returned.

"Anything else I can do for you, sir? Would you like to order your breakfast now?"

Not looking up, Glen said, "No, that's all… Wait, a moment if you please. Can you mail this for me?"

The waiter nodded. "This is the Ritz-Carlton, sir. We have a post drop in the lobby."

Glen handed the envelope to the waiter. The waiter grinned and paused. Glen said, "Sign whatever tip you want to Room 305. I'm not paying for it after all."

"Enjoy your stay on Maui, sir, Saturday's ceremony will be spectacular."

"Spectacular indeed," Glen said to himself as his eyes went to the waves breaking on the rocky shore line. He took another sip of guava juice as he watched the mass of workers prepare the courtyard for the ceremony.

A few minutes later the waiter returned, asked, "Anything else I can do for you, sir?"

Not looking up from the paper, Glen said, "No, that's all."

The waiter sat in the chair across from Glen, asked "Are you sure?"

Shocked at the audacity of the waiter, Glen stood and threw down the paper. He was about to say something, but then abruptly sat back down.

The waiter said, his voice changing as he spoke, "You know, I've had a lot of time to think these past few days. Mostly I asked myself: Why me? Why not some other poor schmuck? That's when I realized there isn't just one box, there's two—ours and theirs."

Glen didn't speak, didn't move.

"Get a new act, Glen, the old one's tired." Scott leaned over and whispered. "If all this goes back to your days with Harry Johnson, you're the one who's over his head, so let's just say it like it is, okay? I want my picture and my name out of the papers. I want it released as a mix-up, deep cover agent gets misidentified as killer, some such, you think something up, you're good at it."

Glen's face went white but not because of what Scott said just then, rather what Scott had said before. "How do you know there are two?"

"Because there are. Two boxes make the pair. It's tit for tat—with you it always is. Don't worry, I won't tell anyone else about your toys that fell into the wrong hands. Do we understand each other?"

"You don't understand, you're taking this all out of context."

"What context would that be? The one where you use information as barter or as a weapon?"

"The boxes were supposed to create a stalemate. Each side had their box. Each box blocked the other and was useless without the other. No one else was supposed to get the boxes or know they existed."

"No one else was supposed to get the A-bomb either."

"The God code was supposed to be self-restricting. One key can't be used without the other and the keys can't be duplicated."

"I know how key encryption works: two keys are required to open the treasure box, but why in the world would anyone create such a treasure box and who would be so arrogant as to believe that if such a thing existed and was discovered that it wouldn't be the number one priority of every psychopath who had an ounce of technical know-how?"

Glen grinned, told himself that nothing Scott said mattered. "Keep your voice down. We're having a nice conversation, aren't we? Nod your head and smile, security will walk away." Scott turned to see what Glen saw. Glen smiled again, stood. "Shall we walk to the beach?"

***

"Give me back the box, Scott. When it goes back in place, all this ends. A cancels B, B cancels A, even if someone else has the code. It's that simple—that's the failsafe."

"You're an arrogant son of a bitch, so sure of yourself that you're out here in broad daylight sipping juice and reading the paper. If I could see through your disguise, what makes you think they can't?"

Glen put his hand on the stone wall, looked out at the waves breaking on the beach for a moment before he turned back to Scott. "Ever see those rats that run around mazes? ... Funny thing, those rats never really know when they're out of the maze. It's just a bit of food at the end that makes them think they're out. Put the food in the middle of the maze and hell, they'll think they're done and they don't care about the maze, only the prize."

Scott pushed away from the wall. "Screw you! When Cynthia and I are both safe and out, I'll send you the box."

"Scott, we're one step away from something that'll make the

Great Depression seem like a picnic and you're going to—"

"Save it, I don't give a damn! Now, you can do whatever you're going to do but I'm going to walk out of here. I'm going to get on a plane. I'm going to get Cynthia. We're going to disappear and you're going to let us."

Glen's anger showed clearly on his face. He felt the hand of God on his shoulder as he leaned close to Scott and said in a low voice, "Remember what happened to John Tippton in the Mid East? By the time we got to him, they'd worked him for seven days and nights. They were giving him shock treatments by then. I found him all wired up to these truck batteries, and he begged me to just put a bullet in him. When I wouldn't do that, he begged me for my gun so he could do it himself. That'll be you, if—"

"If what?" Scott mocked Glen. "Black ops have always been your thing, Glen, only this time it was black boxes. A matched set: They had one; you had the other. Had to have something to replace those missiles after the Cold War, didn't you, you bastard?"

"You don't understand. This isn't—"

"I understand, I understand all too well." Scott took a step away from Glen. "I've got one now and I set the rules. You want to see it again, you let me walk away. When we're safe, you'll get a special delivery."

"What, you came back to make demands? I'm so disappointed. Here, I thought you'd be half a world away by now." Glen raised his hand, fingers outstretched and pointed at Scott's face. He had a small caliber gun hidden within his hand and the muzzle of the gun was now pressed into the eye socket next to the bridge of Scott's nose. "I kill you now, then Cynthia and I will have a chat. Do you think she'd like that? Do you think she'd squeal like a stuck pig? I wonder if I'd kill her after or—"

Unflinching, Scott said, "Pull the trigger, we both die." He nodded to the security personnel that seemed to be everywhere. "I can live with that, can you?"

"I can live with that."

"Bullshit, you're here to do what I didn't. What you didn't do with your bare hands twenty years ago either. You're here to kill him. Kill me and security will be in your face within 30 seconds. As a bonus, that special delivery gets delivered but not where you want it to go."

"You're bluffing."

"Think so?"

"Don't try my patience, Scott."

Scott grinned. "I'm going to step away now. You're going to let me." Scott took a step back, then another. "If anything happens to Cynthia before I return, you'll pray they get you first. Trust me on that."

Glen shouted, "You're making a mistake!"

"Am I?" he squinted, didn't wait for a response. He already knew what Glen would say—a clever lie, a shading of the truth, but never the truth.

He turned and ran back to the hotel. If his luck was holding, there would be a cab waiting in front of the hotel—cabbies would do just about anything for a couple Benjamin Franklins. As he entered the lobby, he tried to remain focused on what he had to do, and getting to the airport and then past the security checkpoints was the least of his worries.

The lobby was crowded. But these weren't typical travelers. Tourists didn't wear Armani business suits in 90 degree heat. He turned to look back as he reached the glass entry doors. Glen hadn't followed; he didn't think Glen would. But more importantly, it appeared no one else had either.

He turned back, opening the door as he went, nearly slamming into a woman in a red dress. The woman pulled back, put up her hands, trying to get out of Scott's way as he rushed out to the waiting cab. Scott stumbled into the woman, his hands going to her waist as he stopped himself. "God, I'm sorry," he said as he stepped away to the cab.

The woman put her hand on Scott's arm as if to push him away. "Don't worry about it, it happens," she said.

Scott took a step away, stopped. The woman's dress showed off every supple curve but it wasn't the curves that caught Scott's attention or the long blond hair. It was the eyes: The eyes never lie.

As he passed the woman, he reached back and grabbed her arm. "Helen?" He said it even though he knew it was impossible, he had seen the bomb explode in Helen's face with his own eyes. He shook his head, closed his eyes, then opened them wide, taking in the sight that he wasn't quite sure was there. "Helen, is that you?"

Upset now, the woman turned back to him. "My name is Jessica, Jessica Wellmen. Please now, let go of me."

He held on, mesmerized by the woman's eyes, but she didn't have to ask again. Security personnel swarmed over Scott from the lobby and from the front of the hotel. Two guys who barely fit in their charcoal gray suits grabbed him from behind and pulled him away.

They tossed him into the drive, near the cab, suggesting he leave quickly. He got in the cab, told the driver to take him to the airport. He didn't look back.

Chapter 22

Baltimore, Maryland
Friday, 28 January

The new butler brought Scott the morning edition of the *Washington Post*. Scott glanced at the front page. Pleased to see there wasn't a word about a financial crisis in any of the headlines, he turned back to Cynthia, smiling, a dumb grin that wouldn't go away. He said, "How do you feel today? It's Friday, January 28th, do you know that?"

Cynthia smiled and blinked her eyes. "I feel," she said, her voice weak and low, but stronger than yesterday and stronger than last Tuesday when she had looked at him and he knew she was past any danger. She patted her belly. "James and I feel."

Scott sucked at the air and looked away. There was no baby, but he couldn't tell her that. Not now, not yet.

"What is it? What's wrong?"

Scott gripped her hand. "There's nothing wrong."

"Don't lie to me, you're not good at it."

Scott moved away from the bed and poured a glass of water, offered it to Cynthia. His hands were shaking. "The doctor said the machines are going tomorrow. Isn't that wonderful?"

"With nurses still watching over me and this—" Cynthia scratched at the IV needle in her hand.

"For a while, yes, but we're free once the machines are gone."

Cynthia looked at him with sincere eyes. "Scott, what aren't they telling me? I hear whispers, the doctor won't talk to me, daddy won't talk to me… You look away."

"Drink this, rest, save your strength." He held the cup. She drank a few sips. He told her, "Close your eyes, I'll be here when you awake."

"Not yet," she said. "I should have listened to you. I should've let Edward take care of everything." Softly she added, "Me and my big head."

"The accident wasn't your fault, the other guy hit you."

"No, I slammed into the truck trying to get away from that black car."

"Black car?"

"The one that kept passing me, stopping in the middle of the road afterward. Crazy guy, told me his name was John and that I had to get out of the car."

"Get out of the car?"

"Yeah, a bomb. Hah!" Cynthia nodded to the Chapstick.

He dabbed the Chapstick carefully to her lips, then kissed her gently, his resolve coming quickly. "I didn't want to tell you this now, but we have to go away."

"A trip now?"

"Yes, a trip. Think of it as a trip, only we won't be coming back for a long time, an extended vacation. Are you okay with that?"

"My knight in shining armor," she whispered. She held his hand for a moment then said, "I'm tired."

"Sleep," Scott told her.

Cynthia closed her eyes. Scott waited until she was asleep before he left the room. As soon as he was in the hall, his calm slipped away. He slammed his fists into the wall, tried to control his anger but couldn't. "Why?" he screamed at deaf walls. "Why?"

The nurse rushed into the hall to see what was wrong. Scott waved her away.

"Quiet," the nurse said as she backed away. "She needs her rest, for her sake as much as the baby's."

Scott's eyes went wide. "Baby?"

The nurse looked at him like he was dimwitted. "Baby James, or so I'm told. She's a fighter, that one, baby going to be strong just like the mom. Don't rightly know if it's a boy. The other one was a boy. We know that, but this one could be a girl. She won't let us check, says she already knows."

"Other one?"

"The baby she miscarried. What, he didn't tell you it was twins? I can understand, 'nough trauma already for everybody."

"He?"

"The granddaddy, Mr. Simons, such a nice man."

Scott changed his mind about letting Cynthia rest and waiting any longer. He asked the nurse, "How much is he paying you?" Before she could answer, Scott said, "I'll double it."

"Double?"

Scott eyes went to the duffle bag on the floor near the foyer. "Hell, if you'll help pack and come with us, you can set the price."

"Where?"

"Somewhere tropical, warm. How does that sound?"

"My Toby, what about my Toby? Can't rightly leave 'im behind."

"Write him a letter. Tell him you'll be back in a few months."

"My Toby can't read, Mr. Evers. Dogs don't read."

"Dog?"

"Rottweiler, hates everybody but me."

"Good, we'll bring him along. How long will it take you to pack everything you need?"

"Few minutes I reckon. Doctor said the machines could go. Just the meds mostly."

Smiling, Scott clapped his hands together, said, "Well, let's get to it."

Minutes later Scott was staring at Cynthia through the rear-view mirror and nodding to the butler who was standing on the lawn as he pulled away from the front of the house. He turned on the headlights, continued around the circle drive.

The front gate moved slowly outward and just as the car started toward the gates, Cynthia opened her eyes and looked up. Scott, still looking at her through the rearview mirror, smiled. "Rest," he said, "Everything's going to be okay now," and then he drove away into the night.

Look for these
Scott Evers Thrillers...

The Cards in the Deck

The Pawns on the Board

The Players in the Game

About the Author

Robert Stanek is the author of many previously published books, including several bestsellers. Currently, he lives in the Pacific Northwest with his wife and children. Robert is proud to have served in the Persian Gulf War as a combat crewmember on an electronic warfare aircraft. During the war, he flew numerous combat and combat support missions, logging over two hundred combat flight hours. His distinguished accomplishments during the Persian Gulf War earned him nine medals, including the United States of America's highest flying honor, the Air Force Distinguished Flying Cross.

As a boy, he dreamed of being a writer. In elementary school, he was a junior editor for the school newspaper. Although he has written many books for professionals since 1994, his works of fiction have quickly become his most popular books. His first novel was Keeper Martin's Tale, which was simultaneously released in adult and children's editions. He describes the book as "a story of mystery, intrigue, magic, and adventure." Many of his other works of fiction are also fantasies, set in incredibly fantastic worlds.

Learn more at
www.reagentpress.com

9 781575 452357